NIGHTFALL

Amelia Doss Series Book 2

ANDRE GONZALEZ

AUDREY BRICE

NIGHTFALL (AMELIA DOSS SERIES, #2)

Andre Gonzalez and Audrey Brice

M4L Publishing, LLC
U.S.A.

"Go on, Ella, ask him out. You've been staring at him every day." Rachelle lightly smacked Ella on the arm, causing her to jump. "Well?"

Ella forced a coy smile. "I would just make a fool of myself."

"So you're going to spend the semester crushing on Jason Pensa from afar when you *could* be his girlfriend?" Rachelle shrugged, her dark brown hair cascading down her shoulders in ringlets. "Suit yourself."

With a heavy sigh, Ella turned to her new friend, catching the scent of the jasmine perfume the girl wore. She cringed. "Of course, I'd like to go out with him, but shouldn't *he* ask me out?"

Rachelle shook her head. "Maybe that's how it is where you come from. But here, it's okay for a girl to ask out a guy. People do it all the time and the world doesn't stop." She leaned toward Ella. "Just go over there and say hi."

"He's with his friends. What if..." *Tyler recognizes me*, she finished silently.

"What if what?"

"What if he turns me down in front of all those people?" Ella gave her the most serious look she could muster.

"Then he's an idiot, and it's his loss," Rachelle said, her voice confident and dismissive.

"Ugh, fine," she said, standing. This was it – the moment of truth. Did she look different now? She no longer had her matted blond hair. Her skin was no longer blotchy. She looked like a normal college student. Picking up her backpack and hoisting it over her shoulder, she took a deep breath. This was the only way she could get close to Tyler, and she'd seen Jason glancing at her in their sociology class several times. "I'm confident. I can ask Jason out."

"Go get 'im, girl," Rachelle whispered, giving her a broad smile and a thumbs up.

She walked toward Jason, Tyler, and a few other guys huddled at one of the cafeteria tables, and when she was less than three feet away, Jason looked up.

"Hi," she said, in the same way she'd heard Rachelle talk for weeks now. "I'm Ella Jones. I'm in your sociology class."

"Ah. Ella," Jason said. He swung around on the stool to face her, revealing the bright white and green sneakers he was wearing. "Yeah, I've seen you in class. What's up?"

"I was just wondering if you'd like to get coffee sometime," she said. On television, coffee was less committal than dinner or an actual date.

"Or we could catch dinner and a movie?" he suggested.

Ella forced what looked like a genuine smile. "That would be great, too."

"But coffee, too," he corrected. He seemed to feel just as awkward about the exchange.

By this time, she was feeling more confident. "After class this afternoon?"

"Absolutely."

She was vaguely aware of Tyler's eyes on her, but she

didn't see any hint of recognition on his face. "Great. See you in class." Then she whirled around and practically ran back to the table where Rachelle was gathering her things. They had American Literature 101 together in fifteen minutes.

"Did you ask?" she asked, her eyes searching over Ella's shoulder. "They're all looking at you, and one of the guys just hit him on the arm." Her brows raised.

A slow smile spread over Ella's lips. That had been a lot easier than she thought. "Yep. Coffee after class today, and possibly dinner and a movie at some other time."

"Damn. You're on fire!"

Ella jumped and looked around at herself.

Rachelle laughed and grabbed her arm. "You take things so literally. You're not really on fire. Don't you have television in the wilds of Wyoming?"

Forcing a smile, Ella followed. But her mind was on Tyler and how she would use Jason to get to him.

FOUR HOURS LATER, SHE SAT ACROSS FROM JASON PENSA as he yammered about sports, parties, television, and a lot of things Ella knew little about. Nor did she care to. Jason annoyed her, but she knew just how important it was to act interested. "So how is living in the dorms?" she finally asked, hoping to not only make an attempt at small talk, but to gain some insight into Tyler and his life in the dormitory.

"Don't you live on campus?" he asked.

She shook her head. "I live with my great-aunt. I was given an exception because she needs daily care."

He gave her a blank look. "I guess that means you won't be having any parties then?" There was a tinge of hope in his voice.

From television, she knew that young people often had

parties, but large gatherings also drew a lot of attention from the police. "No. My aunt is old and…"

"I was only kidding," he said. "You're kind of lucky you don't live in a dorm. I mean, I imagine living with your aunt is probably annoying, but you don't have to contend with roommates and a bunch of rowdy guys on either side of you."

"Your roommate doesn't seem too bad," she said, careful to watch her tone.

"Nah. He seems like a decent enough guy. Kind of quiet in a spooky way." He shrugged.

"Spooky?" She found herself intrigued by such a comment.

"Haunted, or something. I don't know. Like his mind is always someplace else. But deep down, he's a good guy." Jason shrugged again.

Oh, Tyler, have you been thinking of me? she wondered. Ella wanted to grill Jason some more, but it was too soon. She didn't want to seem overly curious about Tyler, since that might trigger a warning, and she had to stay in Jason's good graces in order to remain close. Making Tyler pay in ways he never imagined. She took another sip of her coffee.

"So how are your classes?"

"Fine. And yours?" she asked.

"That doesn't sound like a ringing endorsement for higher education," he said with a chuckle. "What's your major again?"

"English for now, but that might change," she said. None of this prattling was getting her any closer to moving in on Tyler. "It's general core for the first two years, anyway. Plenty of time to decide if I want to change majors."

"Yeah, I guess," he said. A strange look passed over his face.

Inwardly, she winced, because it appeared he was quickly losing interest. "I don't want to talk about classes. I'm sorry. I want to do something fun. I feel like all I'm doing is studying for tests and going to lectures." She forced yet another smile. "I think I'd like to go out with you tonight. I could use a night out," she said, carefully choosing the less formal *night* over *evening*.

The enthusiasm he'd initially had sprang back to his face. "Great! You'll really like my friends. They're cool."

"It sounds fun," she said. Then she glanced at her watch, searching for an excuse to cut their coffee date short. "I have to pick up my aunt's prescription before the pharmacy closes. I'm sorry I have to run off, but when should I meet you at your dorm?"

"Around seven?" he asked.

Getting up, she slung her backpack over her shoulder. "Okay, see you at seven!" Then she walked away, looking back to wave and throw him one final smile. She hurried across campus to her car and got in. "Oh, Aunt Betty, you're even useful in death. And I thought you were just meat," she said to no one, then giggled. Starting the ignition, she headed toward home, and realized she missed her shadow friends terribly. They rarely accompanied her to campus. There weren't enough dark places for them to lurk during the day. They were the only ones she could really talk to. The only ones who understood her. As she drove, a store sign caught her eye. *Frank's Outdoor Center*, it read. Her interest piqued, she pulled into the parking lot. She left with some mountain climbing rope, duct tape, and a fixed-blade folding hunting knife. She smiled at the bag in the passenger seat next to her, then headed toward home again, only to make a quick stop at the pharmacy for some red lipstick. The shade she chose was called Deep Wine. If she was going to win Jason over, it would be with superficial charm, and plenty of makeup. With the help of the Internet, she would make herself irresistible.

Upon arriving home, she did what she usually did. Waved

at the neighbor across the street while he watered his bushes, grabbed the mail, and let herself into the house. The cool silence and darkness greeted her, and so did the shadows.

"Amelia," they said.

"I'm home, but only for a short while," she told them. She dropped her bag from the sporting goods store on one of the chairs, tossed her backpack next to the side table along with her purse and keys, and took the lipstick to the bathroom. A pang of hunger gripped her. She'd forgotten to take a slice of Betty from the freezer, and it wouldn't be thawed in time for her to eat before she went. She certainly didn't want to go out with Jason on an empty stomach. He, or one of his friends, would be too tempting to eat. Clean meat. Instead, she went to the fridge and pulled out one of the steaks she'd bought the night before, gave it a wary second thought, but ultimately devoured it raw over the sink. After cleaning up her face and hands, she made herself a cup of tea.

Unintelligible whispers from the dark recesses of the house filled her ears.

"I have a date. Well, I think it's a date," she casually announced to the shadows. She could feel their eyes watching her, waiting. When they didn't respond, she turned toward the darkness of the hallway where they were culminating into a black, writhing mass. "With Jason. Tyler's roommate."

"Good. Then you can kill him," one shadow snarled.

"Patience, my friends. First, I need to become the boy's one and only love interest so I can get closer to Tyler. Then I can rid the world of Jason Pensa and send his soul to the pits of hell." Her eyes narrowed as her plan came into focus, and a sly smile slid over her balm-covered lips. "I need to be well-liked by his social circle, so when he dies, I'm the poor bereft girlfriend."

"Very good," the shadows cooed in unison.

She got up and retrieved the laptop from her backpack

and returned to her favorite chair. Upon opening, the screen glowed to life. She clicked the Internet icon and the search engine popped up, then she hunted and pecked at the keys with her newly manicured fingertips until she'd typed a single sentence: *Outfits appropriate for a college party.* She clicked on *images.* Rows upon rows of women dressed in modern fashions appeared and she began perusing her choices. She had plenty of clothes in her room to mix and match; surely, she could come up with something. The light outside grew gray as a late afternoon storm rolled in, allowing the shadows, one by one, to slip into the room and surround her.

"You need a place to hide a knife," one of them said.

Ella merely nodded in agreement, her eyes glancing over to the other chair with the bag containing her new folding hunting knife. She got up, took the knife from the bag, and then trotted to her room to try on the outfit she had in mind.

❧

AT FIVE MINUTES TO SEVEN, ELLA, NOW CLAD IN TIGHT jeans and a black scoop-neck blouse covered with a black cardigan, paused at the entrance to Jason and Tyler's dorm and looked up at the building. The horrific idea of people living in such close quarters made her stomach wretch a bit. "A bit like a meat warehouse," she whispered under her breath.

"It's you!" A woman's voice, wavering slightly, came at her from her left.

She turned to see an old woman wearing a long brown, stained coat. A gray, crusty knit cap covered her head. The woman carried a dirty, torn backpack.

"They told me about you," she said, pointing at Ella. "You can't kill me in the light, demon."

Ella felt her face twist into a scowl. She'd rip out the bitch's eyeballs...

"Ella!"

She turned from the old homeless woman to find Jason and Tyler, and a few other guys she didn't know, coming out of the building.

Jason's eyes went wide, and he smiled. "You look... wow."

Focus, she told herself, and threw on a big smile. "This is fun me. Not student me." Then she turned back toward the homeless woman, only to see the woman yards away now, heading in the opposite direction. If she ran across the old bat again, she'd have no choice but to kill her.

"Who was that?"

Ella let out an exasperated sigh. "I don't know. Some homeless person. She was telling me I was the devil or something. It's probably the lipstick."

Jason let out a nervous laugh. "Yeah, campus security really needs to do something about the homeless folks on campus."

His friends, including Tyler, nodded in agreement. Then Jason slipped his arm across her shoulder and they began walking toward the inner city that was downtown Denver. Tyler walked alongside them, right next to Ella, completely unaware that he was less than two feet from Amelia Doss.

❧ 2 ❧

The homeless man gurgled one last time before going limp: his body oozing blood from the knife wounds she'd inflicted upon him. Knives were easier to come by and even easier to hide, but she had to admit that she missed her trusty axe. The shadows, her long-time companions, huddled in around her, whether to obscure her from view or to watch as she ate her prey, she couldn't guess. They always closed in on a kill if it was dark enough. But she was growing tired of the fetid, stinking meat of Denver's homeless. While they made for plentiful, easy prey, she longed for the days of cleaner meat. If Ridgeway had taught her anything, it was that clean meat was more easily missed by the locals and the police always got involved.

For months now, she'd spent her time laying low, away from the long arm of the law. She'd come to Denver because the city had grown since her time, and it was easy to get lost in the crowd. Here, no one knew of her past. There were no legends to precede her, no town museums to alert anyone to her presence. Now that she looked like every other young twenty-something female, no one looked twice at her unless they were a man. Finding a new place to live had taken a little work, but by luck, and by the grace of the shadows and their scouting abilities, she'd found a small house in a suburb outside of Denver, inhabited by an old woman who had no family to speak of. She'd advertised a room for rent in the local paper, and Amelia had responded.

After gathering enough cash begging on a street corner as she'd seen her prey do, she'd rented a room from the woman, and had even let her live for a few months before slaughtering the old bag for her tough, sinuous meat. But not before having learned to drive, getting a complete makeover, and convincing the neighbors that she was Betty's great-niece, Ella, who'd moved here from Wyoming to go to college in Denver. After she'd killed Betty by pushing her down the cellar stairs, an act that had broken the old woman's neck, she'd cut her up and preserved the meat in the freezer. Amelia, now Ella, told the neighbors her great-aunt had flown out to Michigan to stay with an old friend to help her through chemotherapy. The lie had worked, and now, she not only had a house and car, but also received Betty's retirement checks. She had access to Betty's bank account to purchase clothes and other sundries, occasionally buying raw meat and other supplies, which did a good job of thwarting any rumors and making her appear normal. While it was doubtful the ruse would work forever, she figured it would buy her a couple of months. Long enough to do what needed to be done.

Yes, she'd learned a lot in the past few months, including that Tyler Reynolds had been accepted at Denver State University. Small-town papers, like they had in Ridgeway, were the best. Especially when you could just look them up on the computer. Betty had been a kind old woman who'd taught Ella everything about computers and cell phones, and how banks worked. She'd learned how to use a stove, a microwave, the television, and so many other electronic gadgets the world now ran on. The old woman had even helped her fill out her college application, and the Internet had taught her how to fake a high school transcript. Everything appeared to be going so flawlessly, that like most living people, she worried something bad was going to happen at any moment.

She finished her meal and left the homeless man by the railroad tracks, wiping her face and hands before slipping away into the darkness, the shadows following her. They had been quiet tonight.

"When will we get to slice up Tyler?" one of them finally asked.

She gave the shadow the side-eye. "In due time," she whispered. She knew better than to openly talk to the shadows where someone might see her. They would undoubtedly assume she was talking to herself and think her crazy. It wasn't her fault that others didn't see the shadows. They were good at hiding. Just like she was good at hiding who she really was. Inside her mind, her lust for vengeance burned, but she had to be patient. She was willing to endure this new world of sin and perversion to make Tyler pay for the crimes of his kinsman. Though she was more and more convinced that Tyler was just pretending to be Tyler, like she pretended to be Ella Jones. That he was actually Randall Nelson, just like she was actually Amelia Doss.

"You are a sneaky one," she murmured under her breath. She shoved her hands into the pockets of her black hoodie and made her way up another block. Only then would she turn right, go two more blocks, and find herself home. Funny how she thought of the old house as home. Over the summer she'd cleaned all the weeds out of the yard, planted flowers, and tidied things up. It had gone a long way to building good-will with the neighbors.

"Don't forget you told Rachelle that you were going to bring her a copy of *Catcher in the Rye* from the old bitch's library," one shadow reminded her.

She nodded in response. Rachelle was one of her new college friends; another English major she'd met at orientation. But unlike Amelia, Rachelle couldn't get the exception to live off-campus like *Ella* had. After all, *Ella Jones*, while an out-of-state student from Wyoming, was caring for her aging great-aunt. The same Great-Aunt Betty who was allegedly in Michigan, but was actually in the freezer downstairs. The college had found the whole situation endearing and had given her a disability exception for living off-campus. *Ella* had been friendly and kind to Rachelle. After all, she had to have friends if she was going to blend in seamlessly. That they shared a major was only a coincidence.

Upon finally arriving, she slipped the key into the lock and entered the house unseen. She flicked on the living room light before locking the door behind her, then moved to the bathroom and turned on the light there, pausing to look at her reflection in the mirror. She wasn't the same Amelia she had been back in Ridgeway. She was still youthful, but the face that looked back at her was no longer the young woman she once knew. The blood and flesh of her prey, and people's belief in her, had replenished her youthful appearance. She still had the same flawless skin and high cheekbones. But she'd had her hair cut a little shorter and layered, and it had red highlights now. Her eyebrows were no longer unkempt, now shaped thin and clean, and she'd begun wearing makeup to accentuate her features. She looked just like all the other young women she'd seen walking across campus. She'd used the old woman's credit cards to purchase a new wardrobe. No more long, out of fashion dresses. She opted for jeans, blouses, and short skirts—though she still preferred to wear tights with them. There were just some things about the new world she wasn't comfortable with yet, and showing too much of her own flesh was one of them. Though she knew that a time might come when she'd have to lose those inhibitions for the greater good. To kill Tyler Reynolds.

"I wonder how long it took him to learn to blend in with the dross of this culture," she mused into the mirror with narrowed eyes. Her attention traveled from the foreign face in the mirror to the front of her hoodie and she unzipped it, shrugged it off and dropped it in the clothes hamper. She hadn't bloodied it too much. "That will easily come out in the laundry," she said. Then her eyes went to the dark hallway where the shadows lingered, waiting for her to come out of the light. "Well? Anything else I should know?" she asked them.

She could hear them tittering and whispering to one another, but she couldn't make out what they were saying.

Finally, one voice came through loud and clear. "They know who you are," one of them said.

A sly grin slid onto her lips. The homeless knew there was a killer on the loose, as did the police, she imagined, but it was doubtful they knew the name Amelia Doss.

"Of course, they know your name. We've told them. Why do you think your skin is much brighter, your eyes more vibrant?" it asked.

"No one can hear you except for me," she said.

"But some of them can," a smaller shadow said, then giggled like a small child.

The giggle triggered a memory from Amelia's past, but it was only a flash and the bright light of the bathroom caused it to scuttle away into the darkness like a vole scurrying to its hole in the ground. "Well then, if they can, so be it. As long as Tyler Reynolds doesn't know. Not yet. It's not time. I must fully integrate into his group of friends before that can happen." She turned on the shower, adjusting the temperature as hot as her skin would allow, then finished undressing and left the shadows behind the closed shower curtain.

When she finished bathing, she slipped on a nightshirt and did the laundry, then heated a cup of water in the microwave to fix herself a cup of tea. This was her favorite part of the day. While the rest of the world slumbered, she sat in the living room with only a small lamp to illuminate her chair, drinking her tea and going over the coming day's schedule. Getting back to sleeping during the night had taken some doing since she'd always been rather nocturnal. But the rigors of college and maintaining her subterfuge wouldn't allow for her to keep to the darkness. Not this time. This time, the only way she could get close to Tyler was by living in his world, out in the open for all to see. There were things that had to be done. Plans to be made, and Amelia had been trying to learn the fine intricacies of dating, the modern version of a courtship. She'd been watching television shows in hopes that the body language, the modern American dialect, and the etiquette would rub off on her. So far, it seemed to work. Her friend, Rachelle, had noticed nothing amiss, but she had corrected Amelia's pronunciation on occasion, chalking it up to Ella being raised in Wyoming. Amelia never corrected her, just laughed along with Rachelle's ridiculous commentary, and tried to learn from it. In that sense, Rachelle remained valuable enough to keep around, and she'd introduced Amelia to her other friends and made her feel included and liked. Getting beyond her natural shyness had been difficult for Amelia, so she'd been working on that too, with Rachelle's help. Modern women were boisterous and didn't do what men told them. That was a trait Amelia admired, and she was getting better at it, but sometimes there was a tinge of viscousness to her voice when she spoke up. That was something that needed work as well, along with speaking to men with a tender touch. She'd been practicing on the shadows.

"How will we know when to kill him?" one shadow asked, pulling her out of her reminiscence.

"In due time," she said, a flash of annoyance in her voice. Then she smiled and pulled her legs up underneath her on the chair. She took another sip of her tea and cringed. It was bitter. She made a quick mental note to try a different brand next time she went to the grocery store, a place that smelled of putrid meat and rotting vegetation. How anyone could enter those large buildings without it turning their stomach, she didn't know. It made her queasy to go in there, but she forced herself to. "Perhaps I should do more Internet research," she said aloud to no one, not really having any idea what she should research. She'd looked up just about everything.

"Ways to slaughter the damned?" one of the shadows asked.

The shadows were becoming tiresome with all their yammering. Sometimes their voices and constant suggestions to kill or maim made it hard for her to concentrate, let alone fit in and practice being Ella. "No. Not tonight," she told them, her voice firm. "Perhaps I should just go to bed. I have an early morning," she said, getting up from the chair. She picked up the plain white mug and took it to the kitchen sink, rinsing it out gingerly. Grabbing the copy of *Catcher in the Rye* from the bookshelf to stow it in her backpack, she then turned off the lights and headed upstairs. She was tired and needed all the sleep she could get, because fitting into Tyler's world required a lucid and well-rested mind.

As she turned out the lights in her bedroom and slipped beneath the cool sheets, she heard a click as her door closed. From the hallway, "Good night, Amelia," said one of the shadows in a low, guttural voice.

She smiled. "Good night."

16

❧ 3 ❧

Tyler Reynolds snapped his laptop shut and leaned back in his desk chair, gazing out the window to the bustling campus of Denver State University. He had moved to the capital city in early August to get acclimated to his new dorm, school, and roommate. So far everything had checked out just fine, setting up what he hoped would be a productive and fun first semester of college life. And most importantly, no one in the big city knew who Amelia Doss was, or could even point out Ridgeway, Colorado on a map.

He had debated between Denver State or the closer-to-home Western Plains College, but decided putting some distance between himself and Ridgeway was what he truly needed for a fresh start. This allowed him to limit his trips home to the major holidays, compared to Western Plains, where he could have gone home every weekend if he pleased.

Not all was lost from home, either. Tyler's best friend, Danny Espinoza, decided to attend Denver State, too. He had already moved down a couple weeks prior to Tyler, needing to get settled in sooner and begin training for his new job as a campus security guard.

They had dinner with each other at least three times each week, and the conversation always seemed to drift back to that horrific evening when they had run Amelia Doss out of Old Lady Myers' basement, saving Tyler's mother.

His eyes fell upon the notebook that he kept on the back corner of his desk, stuffed with notes on their extensive research into Amelia's life and all the hell she had unleashed on Ridgeway over a century ago. The memories of that fateful night where his mother would have ended up murdered had plagued his thoughts ever since leaving Ridgeway. What if Amelia returned while he was gone and butchered everyone who had been involved in chasing her away? He thought of his parents, Sheriff Abbott, and Danny's parents to start, but it branched out much further than he realized. He had made a conscious decision to bring the notebook with him to college, not believing he'd need it, but not wanting to be caught without it, either. *Better safe than sorry,* he reminded himself again.

The doorknob jiggled before swinging open to reveal Tyler's roommate, Jason Pensa, filling the doorway with his broad, athletic body, his pearly white grin greeting Tyler. "Hey, bro, how are things?" he asked, closing the door behind him and stepping all the way in, tossing a gym bag on his bed.

"Pretty good. How was working out?"

"Another day, another sweat. No complaints from me."

Tyler grabbed a paper and tossed it on top of the Amelia Doss notebook to keep it out of sight. While he and Jason were still in the early phases of learning about each other, the story of Amelia would remain something he'd bring up after they had developed full trust, if such a point existed.

"What do you have going on tonight?" Tyler asked. It was

Friday, and that surely meant Jason had a couple of parties to attend later in the evening.

Jason sat down on his bed and took off his shoes, slipping them back onto the shelf that he kept elevated above his bed. The eighteen-year-old from California had an odd obsession with basketball shoes, displaying only a portion of his prized collection that contained mostly older Jordan brand sneakers, and Air Force Ones in every color of the rainbow. While Tyler didn't have a fashionable bone in his body, he couldn't help but occasionally admire the collection.

"I'm going to a party off-campus," Jason said. "Gonna shower up and get ready for the night. Probably grab some pizza before—would you and Danny want to come with?"

"Oh, I don't know."

"There are going to be some fine hunnies at this party—you never know who you could meet. The future Mrs. Reynolds, perhaps?" Jason raised his eyebrows while a grin spread across his face.

The two were still in the phase of feeling the friendship out, inviting each other to everything, even if they didn't really want to. Tyler wasn't one for the party scene—at least on such a regular basis like Jason—but he had no plans and couldn't think of a viable excuse to talk himself out of it.

"Okay. I'll have to see if Danny is free, but either way, I'll go." *Danny better be free—I don't really want to go alone.*

Jason grinned as he stood back up, taking his shirt and tossing it into his hamper at the foot of his bed. "I look forward to it. I'm gonna go clean up if you wanna call Danny and let him know the plans." He paused and put his hands on his hips. "Our first night out. Of many to come."

Jason disappeared into the bathroom and left Tyler alone at his desk again. *I don't know about 'many to come', but it will be nice to get out of the dorm and interact with others.* Tyler's stomach fluttered with nerves at the thought of going to a party.

Ridgeway wasn't much of a party town, and considering how small it was, it had been nearly impossible for small gatherings with friends to have any alcohol present. He'd had sips of his father's beer from time to time, but had never been around a plethora of liquor—and drunken fools—like he expected to encounter tonight.

His expectations had only been formed from what he saw in movies, and while he doubted all college parties reflected Hollywood's depiction, he suspected a fraction of it had some truth. Tyler never had much of a problem with peer pressure and had also never been drunk. He wanted to try it at least once to see what all the hype was about, but debated if this first night out with Jason was the best time for such an experiment.

"I'd rather try it in the dorm, with Danny," he whispered under his breath, already trying to figure ways to get out of the inevitable offer of a drink at the party. Tyler shook his head, frustrated. It was times like these when he missed his old friend, Bryson. Being a popular jock with a wide range of friends, Bryson had served as a natural bridge between Tyler and other kids he wouldn't normally spend time with. He had a way of connecting with people from all backgrounds, an ability that Tyler admired and considered Bryson's greatest trait.

He wondered if Jason would fill a similar role, but doubted it, seeing as they had yet to truly get to know each other.

You're worrying too much, he told himself. *This is the kind of stuff that makes no one want to spend time with you. Just try to relax and go with the flow, live in the moment and stop worrying about what happens next.*

Tyler could hear his mother's voice echoing in his mind, always the one to push him out of his comfort zone with social interactions. But she wasn't physically here. She had no way of knowing about the party, and therefore couldn't try to persuade him to go.

He swiveled around in his chair and grabbed the Amelia notebook, flipping it open and splaying it across his desk. He needed something to take his mind off the growing anxiety he had now developed and wanted the touch of something familiar to set his mind at ease.

Newspaper clippings, article printouts, and photocopies of old black-and-white pictures splayed across the open file. He had intentionally kept the more graphic images in the back to avoid them accidentally being seen—even by himself. For now, he stared at the map of Ridgeway, circles all over town signifying locations of interest as they had tried to piece together a pattern for Amelia's past murders. His eyes narrowed on a star that marked his home, and he couldn't help but wonder what his parents were doing at this exact moment.

They sometimes got off work early on Fridays and were likely planning where to go out for dinner. Neither of his parents were fond of cooking on weekends. He could imagine the smells of pizza dough and fresh baked bread at their favorite Italian restaurant, a line always out the door on Friday nights as it had become a local treasure over its decades in business.

He wondered what Sheriff Abbott was up to, the two having spoken many times over the summer, but not once since Tyler's arrival at college. The sheriff had become a prominent figure in Tyler's life—a natural occurrence, he supposed, after hunting down a serial killer raised from the dead. Last he had heard, the sheriff was ready to take a long overdue vacation, needing time away to unwind from what was surely the most chaotic times to have stricken Ridgeway since Amelia's original attacks a century ago.

Tyler heard the shower turn off in the bathroom, and

snapped the notebook shut again, shoving it back to its corner. He had already felt his mind drifting back into the darkness that was Amelia Doss, his heart simultaneously growing homesick. He had forgotten to call Danny and quickly picked up his cell phone to dial him.

"What's up, Ty?" Danny greeted, the steady clicking of gum being chewed filling Tyler's ear.

"I'm going out tonight with Jason—was hoping you might be free to join me."

"Tyler Reynolds going to a party with people he doesn't know?" Danny chuckled. "I never thought I'd see the day. Afraid I can't—working the late shift tonight, so I'll be strolling through campus well after the sun goes down."

"Damn, was afraid of that. It's okay, I figured this would happen at some point, might as well get it out of the way."

"Don't be afraid of having some fun, Ty. I know you— once school starts, you'll be buried under assignments and will probably never blow off any steam. Take advantage now while you can."

Danny had really opened up since arriving at college, likely relieved to be out from the strict rules and household that his parents had kept him under in Ridgeway. Tyler saw his friend become more outgoing and open-minded, overall loosening up during their couple of weeks on campus.

"I guess. Well, I better get ready for the night. I'll talk to you tomorrow."

They hung up and Tyler tossed his phone on the desk, disappointed he'd already committed to going with Jason before confirming with Danny. Somewhere in his subconscious he likely wanted to go, regardless of Danny's plans.

Jason stepped out of the bathroom, still topless, his hair slicked back with moisture. "You be ready in about an hour?" he asked, staring Tyler up and down, urging him to change his outfit without saying the words aloud.

Tyler nodded, getting up and deciding to take a shower himself. He had only brought a couple of nicer outfits to the dorm, figuring he'd have some sort of event come up that required one. "Give me fifteen minutes and we can head out."

He went to the bathroom and never saw the old newspaper clipping of the bloody axe sticking out from his notebook's edge.

❈   4   ❈

Danny Espinoza made his rounds across the campus of Denver State University. It was approaching 9 P.M. and he still had two more hours on his security shift until he'd get to crawl back into bed and have to wake up for the early shift in the morning. The newbies were handed the worst schedule until classes began, then his shifts would be planned around his school schedule. Until then, he had no choice but to endure late night and early mornings filled with plenty of energy drinks that he knew were not good for him, and eating meals at the oddest of hours.

He had already come to dread the start of a shift, no matter its start time. But once he arrived and walked his first route of the day, he quickly fell into the grace of solitude and getting lost in his thoughts. They filled his first week on the job with learning the route and other duties to handle, but now that he was on his own, he found his appreciation growing with each passing day. The job leant itself to allow him plenty of free time to do homework when the time came. More than enough time, in fact, that he decided he'd finally write a screenplay, something that had been gnawing at him ever since leaving high school behind.

He had mulled over several ideas to develop, but none ever came to fruition. Until encountering Amelia Doss. Ever since seeing her in person and witnessing up close her dead eyes, cold flesh, and rotten teeth, Danny had fallen into a complete obsession with horror and the macabre. He brushed up on horror films from Hitchcock, Carpenter, and Craven, all the way through the newer generations that were much more accessible thanks to modern day streaming apps. He fell into the worlds of Stephen King and Dean Koontz, absorbing everything he could about the genre from those who had a proven track record of mastering it.

His screenplay was underway, and it centered on none other than Amelia Doss. Everyone loved a spooky story set in a small town, so he never really felt he was exercising any creative muscles, but rather stuck to telling something he had lived through. Even the dirty details from the 1920s came naturally to him, considering he had once fully immersed himself in the research from that era. He knew the story inside and out, and just needed to find the best way to lay it out in a way that people would enjoy.

If he wasn't physically writing the screenplay in the security office, he was thinking of all the possibilities while strolling around campus. His mind became fully consumed with the story, and even when he went back to his dorm at the end of another long night, exhausted and mentally worn out, his head would hit the pillow and he'd be wide awake, more ideas swirling in his mind like a vicious hurricane.

"Amelia Doss," he muttered to himself as he passed the university's dining hall. "I'm gonna transform you from my biggest fear into my greatest accomplishment."

He passed a couple of students sitting on a bench, their tongues down each other's throats as they remained oblivious to Danny and the rest of the world around them. He had never been in love—not so much as allowed to go on a date, thanks to his strict mother—but hoped for the opportunity to meet someone and strike up a relationship now that he had total freedom in college. He had already taken a liking to one of his new coworkers, a fellow freshman by the name of Chrissy, but understood she was in a complicated relationship. He'd have to wait until they worked a full shift together to find out what exactly was going on and decide if the situation was worth pursuing.

Until then, it would be that same steady rotation of late-night burgers and horror movies until falling asleep. His parents paid extra for him to have a dorm room to himself, something he had argued against initially, but had since come to enjoy, especially after hearing of the roommate Tyler had been paired up with. He could blare music as loud as he wanted, open the shades as early as he needed, all without having to consider someone else's life. He had wanted to live with Tyler, but Danny's mother refused to allow such a thing, citing Tyler as a dangerous influence on her son, despite the two having been friends since elementary school.

Danny moved along, leaving the couple to enjoy themselves, and spotted a group of rabbits dashing across the courtyard opposite the dining hall. He followed the rabbits with his eyes until they disappeared around the corner of the building. Further up lay a homeless man on the next bench. Danny's heart rate immediately increased upon seeing him, realizing he had his first encounter ahead of him. They had mentioned in his training that it was common for homeless people to wander onto campus and find a place to sleep. Being located downtown made this a weekly occurrence. He had learned it was rare for any of them to cause a scene once asked to leave campus, most happy to do so, understanding they were only camping out until getting caught.

Danny took slow steps to the man who lay on his side, a dusty green jacket draped over his side, and what appeared to be a grocery bag full of socks serving as a pillow. He patted his pepper spray and baton to make sure they were within proper reach, just in case.

"Excuse me, sir," Danny called out, deepening his voice to add an intimidation factor he was aware he lacked.

The man didn't move and even let out a soft snore. Danny took a step closer and saw the man's gray hair spraying out from under a maroon beanie like broom bristles, most of it matted against his sweaty cheeks.

Danny cleared his throat and called out louder. "Sir, you need to leave the campus . . . please."

Still no response, so Danny pulled out his baton and used it to poke the sleeping man in the arm.

His eyelids fluttered as he stirred awake, sitting up with a hoarse grunt, muttering, "What the hell, kid?"

"Sir, I'm sorry to disrupt your sleep, but you know you can't do that here on campus. I need to ask you to leave the premises."

The man let his head bob around, still a bit dazed as he came to. He looked around as if he were expecting someone else to appear out of the shadows, and this caused Danny to tighten his grip on the baton.

"Look, young man, I know you're just doing your job, and I respect that, but you have to let me stay here tonight."

Danny stared into the man's eyes, seeing a certain uneasiness swimming behind them. Was the man hiding from someone? If that was the case, he couldn't allow him to stay on campus. The trouble would just eventually end up here, and Danny would lose his job for allowing such an event to unfold.

"I'm sorry, sir, but we can't allow any non-students to loiter on campus."

"I can't go back there," the man said, shaking his head. "She finds us in the alleys and parks. I'll never sleep if I have to go back. Please, I'm so tired. It's been four days since I've slept at night. I promise I'll be gone when the sun comes up."

Danny looked around to see if there was anyone else nearby, finding that the kissing couple had left their bench, leaving Danny alone with the homeless man. "Sir, please. If you won't leave, I have to call the police. I really don't want to get them involved." He considered his next words before continuing. "I'm new to this job and would appreciate your help."

This earned a small grin from the man, who stood on his feet, the bag of socks now clutched in his grip. "Look, son, I don't mean you any trouble, but I'm safe here. I'm making plans to leave this town—I just need one more night and wish to stay here where I won't get hurt."

Danny lowered the baton, sensing that the man was more scared than him. "Is someone after you?"

The man lowered his head, concealing his eyes from Danny's view. "She's after all of us," he said softly, as if not wanting to be heard. Danny glanced around again, certain someone was going to barge out of the shadows and attack this man. "I've lost four friends in the last two weeks and have heard stories of others gone missing."

"Someone is attacking homeless people?" Danny asked, growing a bit frustrated at the need to pull facts out of the man.

"Murder!" the man snarled. "Murder! An attack would be nice. One of my friends had his throat ripped out, another had his leg shredded to pieces like it had gone through a meat grinder. Others haven't been seen, but we know it was her. The girl in the shadows!"

He abruptly shot up his hand, pointing to the vast darkness behind the bench. Danny recoiled and whipped his baton back in front of him, ready to defend himself.

The man chuckled at this and continued his rant. "Son, you think the girl in the shadows is afraid of that little stick?! She will eat it, then eat your eyeballs right out of your face. If you want to stay safe, the best thing to do is stay inside."

Adrenaline flooded into Danny, his fingertips pulsing against the baton that suddenly felt useless in his hand, like a remote control with dead batteries. It had become increasingly clear the man was delusional, or perhaps high on hallucinogens. There had no been disturbances on campus since Danny had arrived, yet here was this man claiming a 'girl in the shadows' was going around killing innocent people.

"Do you want me to help report these murders to the police?"

The man threw his head back and howled to the night sky, a sound that sent chills up Danny's back. "Young man, the police don't give a *shit* about us. Every dead bum is one less problem they have to worry about. You can tell the cops if you'd like, but they'll probably take a week before deciding to come out and talk to us. Who knows how many more of us will be dead by then? That's why I'm getting the hell out of town tomorrow."

"And you don't know who is behind these murders?"

He shrugged. "Stories have been going around, but nobody knows how true they are. Multiple people have claimed to see her. She has long black hair and carries around a knife. That's all anyone has made out. Cops won't be able to do much with that, either. We've accepted we're on our own, and that's why a lot of us are leaving—been saving up the pennies we collect to buy a bus ticket out of town. I'm gonna take my chances in Phoenix—better winter weather."

Danny took a step back and wondered why these types of murders so close to campus hadn't been reported. Was this really the normal precedent for the homeless community? Surely someone out there fought for their rights and fair representation. He understood how fear could serve as a silencer, having gone through a similar experience in Ridgeway with Amelia.

"Okay, sir, I'll help you. You need to leave this area, but there is another bench on the south side of the soccer field. It's in the dark and the cameras won't pick you up. Stay there for the night and be gone by sunrise."

"Thank you, young man," he replied with a wide grin. "God bless you. You may be saving my life, and I'll always remember you for it."

The man nodded before collecting his things and leaving toward the soccer field on the opposite end of the campus.

As Danny found himself alone again, he considered the man's intense story and the girl in the shadows. The description, while brief and inconclusive, struck a particular nerve within. The thought crept into his mind that it sounded awfully similar to Amelia Doss.

"Impossible," Danny said. "She would never make it this far from Ridgeway."

He returned to the security office to work on his screenplay for the rest of his shift.

§   5   §

With school now in full swing, Tyler spent his evenings in his dorm, completing homework and writing papers. He had the luxury of not needing to work like Danny, since his parents offered to cover all expenses during his first year of college, citing a need for him to focus exclusively on school and achieve the best grades possible.

He had never been more grateful for someone else's generosity. He already had four papers due for different classes, not to mention six books to read and study for upcoming exams. Homework, plus an hour-long dinner break, usually concluded around nine o'clock when Tyler slipped on his headphones and zoned out to Netflix until falling asleep around eleven. He had no idea how a job would fit into such a chaotic schedule and admired Danny for handling it all so well.

Jason was out most nights lately, spending time with Ella at her place off-campus. Apparently, she lived with a relative who was currently out of town, though Jason hadn't offered more details. For the past week, Tyler felt like he was living alone, seeing Jason only for a few minutes as he came to stuff new outfits into his overnight bag and head right back to Ella's place. They had all gone out together on a couple of group outings and got along just fine. But Tyler figured they were still in the honeymoon phase of their relationship and required all the alone time they could get. With Ella having the house to herself, that became the natural spot for Jason to spend his free time. Tyler was sure that would change once Ella's relative came back from wherever they were, so he tried to enjoy it for as long as it lasted.

Tyler had ordered Chinese takeout for dinner, a long night still ahead with his books splayed across the desk. He pushed them back to make room for his food and flipped on the TV that was airing an edited version of *Halloween 4* to provide some background noise while he ate.

Not long into his meal, his cell phone buzzed, and he picked it up after seeing Danny on the caller ID. "Hey man, how are things going?"

"They're okay, Ty," Danny replied, his voice distant and distracted. "I just got off the phone with my mom."

"Is everything okay?"

"No." Danny paused, and Tyler could hear his heavy breathing from the other end of the line. "She told me that Bryson's grave was dug up last night, and they found his coffin empty."

Tyler jumped out of his chair, chopsticks falling to the floor as he started pacing the room. "It can't be *her* . . . can it?" he asked, eyes shooting to the notebook that was currently buried under a pile of textbooks.

"I don't know, but who else could it be? Do you really think some kid would do this as a prank?"

"Maybe someone from one of the schools that Bryson had beaten in football? Shit, I just don't know. Has Sheriff Abbott said anything?"

"His office has only released a statement that they are investigating the matter. Nothing else. He won't say anything about Amelia—he knows we need to keep what happened as big of a secret as we can. If he mentions her, the entire town will spiral out of control. But I think she's back, Ty."

"I agree. She had only run away—we know she wasn't gone for good. It was only a matter of time."

"Yeah, and she waited until we left. We're the ones who know everything about her—more than anyone else in Ridge-way. What are we supposed to do—go back home this weekend?"

"I'm not sure that's a good look, either. Maybe we should call the sheriff and speak to him. He'll tell us more than what he's leaked to the public."

"I can try him later. Where would she even take Bryson's body? Back to that fucking mine?"

"I'm sure that's the first place the sheriff will look. I'll call my parents and see what they have to say—maybe they've noticed something around town that no one else is talking about."

"You do that. I'm gonna look back through my notes and see if there was anything about Amelia digging up old graves in the past—I feel like I read about it at some point."

"Okay, let me know what you find. And Danny . . . stay safe out there."

They hung up and Tyler shuffled to the window for a look outside. Just hearing about Amelia and Ridgeway planted a whole new wave of fear and paranoia in his mind. Knowing she was alive had long been something that kept him up at night, but hearing this news of Bryson's grave disturbed him to the bone. It had to be her. Taunting them. Perhaps it was a mindgame she was playing to lure them back home—that certainly seemed like a stunt she would attempt after sweeping the town and not finding either of the boys who had run her out of Old Lady Myers' house on that fateful night.

"I dare you to try," Tyler whispered, looking to the campus with scattered students going about their day. He couldn't help but wonder what would happen if Amelia had somehow tracked him and Danny down. What sort of damage would she wreck on an entire college campus? Doing so would be irresponsible on her part. She may have gotten away with her senseless murders in Ridgeway, but trying to duplicate that scene in the big city would prove impossible. Cameras covered every square foot of campus, not to mention the Denver police station one mile up the road. She'd never corner Tyler alone, unless he was the one to open his door for a stranger.

Startling him out of his daydreams, the door jiggled and swung wide open as Jason stepped in, his hair a frazzled mess, dark bags under his eyes.

"My God, what happened to you?" Tyler asked, stepping away from the window and returning to his chair.

Jason chuckled, a drunken grin on his face. "I don't get much sleep these days. Ella is an animal in bed, and never wants to sleep. She's like a machine I can't keep up with."

Tyler snorted. "Is that a problem?"

"Not in itself, but damn, I just want to get at least one six-hour stretch of sleep. This chick wakes me up every two hours in the middle of the night."

"So things are getting serious, it sounds like."

Jason nodded. "I hope you don't mind, but I gave her my spare key to the dorm."

Tyler's stomach sunk. He had no issue with Ella on a personal level, but didn't want to walk on eggshells in his own place if she could enter the dorm at any moment.

"Well, Jason, I do mind, actually. This should have been something we discussed. This is *our* place, not hers."

Jason raised his hands, clearly lacking the energy to have this conversation. "Look, I doubt she'll even be here much, if at all. We have a good thing going at her place."

"Then do you have a key to her place?"

Jason shook his head. "She doesn't have a spare copy, but said she'll make me one."

Tyler squirmed in his chair, fighting off the anger that was trying to creep into the rest of his body. "This isn't cool, man. It might not seem like a big deal to you because you're never here anymore, but I am. I study here, eat here, sleep here. What if I walk out of the shower and she's here?"

"Okay, look, I think you're overreacting a bit."

"No! We pay the room-and-board here, not her. I don't care how often she comes over, but she should have to knock, not just stroll in like she owns the place."

"Okay, I'll tell her to knock."

"Then she doesn't need the key. Just take it back."

Jason crossed his arms and frowned. "I'm starting to think this is personal. Is there something wrong with Ella? Because I think very highly of her, so choose your words carefully."

Tyler's jaw hung open before he continued. "Are you kidding me?! This isn't personal, it's about the principle. I just told you I don't care how often she's here. *She* shouldn't have a key, and *you* shouldn't have done this without discussing it with me first. This is my place of privacy, and I shouldn't have to worry about someone walking in at any moment."

Jason nodded. "Okay, I hear you. I'll talk to her about getting the key back. Sorry, I didn't think this was a big deal."

"Thank you," Tyler said, feeling some relief for the first time since Danny had called. "I think Ella is awesome, and I'm happy things are going so well for you two. I just need to have one place where I can be myself and not have to worry about outside factors."

"I can appreciate that. Shit, I might have to tell her we

need to spend some nights here, just so she'll let me sleep, knowing you're in the room."

Tyler laughed. "Sounds like that might not be enough to stop her. Honestly, though, if you guys spend time here and want me to leave, just say the word, assuming it's a reasonable hour, and I'll go to Danny's."

Jason sat on his bed and let his shoulders slouch. "You're a good guy, Tyler. I'm sorry I did this. I suppose I'm not thinking straight."

"Well yeah, you're in love and sleep-deprived. That's a nasty combination."

They shared a laugh. "You and Danny still coming with us to the party?"

"Sure are. Looking forward to it."

Danny had a rare Friday night off work and expressed his desire to go out, needing to get off-campus as the first weeks of school and work were taking their toll on his psyche. Tyler had also found from his first party with Jason that there were others like him who occasionally attended. Off-campus house parties had a more laidback ambiance compared to the ragers that occurred at the frat houses and some of the dorms. People mingled and exchanged pleasant conversation, not at all the shitshow Tyler had expected. And now, with an opportunity to go with his best friend, he somewhat looked forward to it.

"Love to hear it," Jason said, tipping over and lying down. "I told Ella I needed to come get new clothes for the week. Think I might nap for an hour before going back. Wake me, will you?"

Tyler checked the time on his phone and grinned. It wasn't even seven o'clock yet—he hadn't finished dinner after the distractions. Yet, Jason was already snoring, out cold on top of his bed, his arms splayed lifelessly in opposite directions while his mouth hung open. "Yeah, I'll wake you, big guy."

Tyler spun around to his desk, picked up his chopsticks, and finished dinner. He hadn't expected a fight with his roommate so early in the semester, but supposed it was good to get it out of the way and, fortunately, resolved. His anger had distracted him from the fact that Bryson had been dug up in Ridgeway, but as he continued dinner, the reality crept back into his thoughts. He'd never be able to truly shake her from his mind, but Tyler knew Amelia was alive, and she wasn't done with what she came back from the dead to do.

❦   6   ❦

"A night out will do you some good," Tyler said with a raised eyebrow.

Danny wasn't so sure. He'd been working long hours between his classes and the security office. "Yeah," he finally agreed and followed Tyler up the walkway toward the house. Partygoers spilled out onto the lawn and from inside like the house's entrails, and they could faintly hear the music. "Must have some thick walls," he mumbled.

"Loosen up. You've been working yourself to the bone," Tyler said in a last-ditch effort to get Danny to relax.

He drew in a deep breath and nodded. "You're right, I need to just chill."

"Oh, here come Jason and Ella," Tyler said, waving at them as they came down the sidewalk. "Hey, you two!"

Ella waved back.

Danny's stomach twisted a bit. He didn't know what it was, but something wasn't right about Ella. He'd always had a sixth sense about people. He could tell if someone was lying or being genuine, and even if they had ulterior motives. Of course, it could have been that she was just weird. It didn't help that he'd been shying away from women lately. Especially after the incident with the homeless guy. What the hell had he been so scared of? *Amelia Doss*, came his mind's reply. He shuddered and pulled his jacket around himself. "Let's get inside. It's getting cold out here."

"Hi, guys," Ella greeted. She had a strange, plastic smile like gymnasts had when they finished their routine and threw their arms and hands up in the air.

Danny forced himself to smile, if only for the sake of fitting in. "Hey."

He let all three go ahead of him, then followed them into the party. Like everyone else, they pushed through the dizzying maze of people to the alcohol. Yes, they were all underage, but they'd walked here, not driven, and unless the cops showed up, what harm would it do? All college students had a beer now and again, and Danny had already told himself he was only going to have one, maybe two beers. Certainly not enough to get drunk. He'd even eaten two small bags of Doritos and a Hot Pocket beforehand to ensure he wasn't drinking on an empty stomach. He didn't want to take any chances at running into whoever the homeless around Denver were afraid of. Not blind stinking drunk, anyway.

"Security! Security!" someone screamed beside him. Danny jumped, his senses alert, his heart thrumming like a drum in his chest. He turned toward the voice. The guy and his friends laughed. "Dude, you're not here to break up the party, are you?"

Danny held up his hands. "I'm not here in an official capacity, or as a chaperone."

There was more laughter before the big guy with the buzzcut said, "Cool, man!"

He turned back toward the kitchen and the alcohol to find Jason and Ella had already grabbed their drinks. Tyler was opening a beer, so Danny hurried to join him.

Once Ella and Jason disappeared into the crowd, Danny bit the bullet. "So, what do you think of Ella?"

Tyler took a swig of his beer, scrunching his face in a way that showed he didn't really like the taste. "What do you mean?"

"I don't know. There's something... about her." He shrugged, trying to play it off. He knew that with college, Tyler would make new friends, but he didn't want to risk their friendship by being overly critical, either. Good friends were hard to find, and Tyler was his best friend.

"She seems okay." The way Tyler said it, though, suggested he wasn't particularly thrilled. "Why? You into her?"

Danny almost swallowed his beer down the wrong hole. After a quick cough to clear his airway, he shook his head. "No. Nothing like that. I just think there's something odd about her."

"She's from Wyoming," Tyler said, as if that explained everything.

This earned him a puzzled look from Danny. "What's wrong with people from Wyoming? I have a cousin who lives up there, and he's not weird."

"No, I mean, she's sheltered, maybe?" Tyler shrugged.

Danny nodded. Maybe that was it. Maybe not. There was something familiar about Ella and her awkwardness, but he couldn't quite place his finger on it. "Could be," he said. "Well, should we socialize?"

Tyler chuckled. "Yeah, probably."

Together, they moved into the party, the music blaring, and a few attractive women dancing. Danny found himself a suitable spot in a corner where he could see everyone. That seemed safer, and he could people-watch.

"You don't dance?"

He turned toward the voice to find a beautiful dark-haired girl standing beside him nursing what appeared to be a hard lemonade. She was short, but thin, and had sharp features. "No. I don't."

"I'm Marie," she said, holding out her hand.

Danny grabbed it and shook. "Danny Espinoza." In that moment, he never realized just how out of place he felt.

"Is it true you work campus security?" she asked, still trying to make small talk.

"I do."

"What's your major?"

"Still deciding." It's not that he didn't find her attractive or didn't want to talk to her, he just had a lot on his mind. *Maybe after I finish this beer, I'll be able to relax a little*, he thought. "You?"

"Right now, it's a toss-up between sports medicine and business." She paused. "First college party?"

His eyes went wide. "Do I look that uncomfortable?"

A light, lyrical laugh came out of her mouth. "No, not at all. You're just not crouched down with your guy friends scoping out chicks or talking about sports."

Danny looked around the room, finding Tyler crouched down with a group of guys, talking about baseball. He certainly seemed to try harder to fit in.

"With work and classes, I rarely have a night off to go out," he explained. In his back pocket, his phone buzzed. He pulled it out and glanced at the screen. It was the campus security office. "Son-of-a-bitch. Sorry, work," he said. Dodging people and moving back to the front porch, he begrudgingly answered.

"Danny! Can you come in tonight? Gavin called out." It was his supervisor, Mr. O'Brien.

He fought back a groan. "I'm actually out right now and it would take me a few hours to get back to campus, get changed, and report," he lied.

"Well, I thought I'd try. You know how it is. Weekend,

parties everywhere." Mr. O'Brien chuckled. "You're probably at one of those yourself."

"Yeah. A friend had a few people over," he lied again, feeling a pang of guilt in his stomach. Truth was, he really could have used the extra cash, but this was his first real night off in weeks.

"Well, have a good time and see you next shift." The line went dead on the other end.

Danny shook his head at the phone.

"Penny for your thoughts," she whispered into his ear.

He jumped, his heart racing in his chest. It was Ella. "You scared the shit out of me. Don't sneak up on people like that."

She laughed. "I didn't realize I had." Then she narrowed her eyes. "You're awfully jumpy. Everything okay?"

"Yeah. Work call." He swallowed the lump forming in his throat. Dread washed over him, and he felt separated from the herd. "Having fun?"

"I'm enjoying this... beer," she said with an odd grin. "You?"

He nodded and gave her a tight smile. "You think the beer is good, try the whiskey."

A slow smile spread over her lips. "I'm not *a fan*, as they say."

Well, that was an awkward turn of phrase, he thought. "Should we go back in? Can I get you another beer?"

If he didn't know any better, he would have thought she looked surprised at his suggestion. "Yes."

He beckoned her to follow with a wave of his hand. "Come on." He led the way, parting the sea of people with, "Coming through!"

Ella was right behind him, her hand on his shoulder so she wouldn't get left behind.

The intensity of her grip sent a chill down his spine, but he ignored it and pressed on, soon making it back to the kitchen and the beer, thankful when her thin hand released its hold on his shoulder. He grabbed her another and opened it. "Here you go."

"Thanks, Danny. You are a lot different than I've heard." She smiled again. There was definitely something off about her smile. Jason came up behind her and wrapped his hands around her waist, causing a flash of anger in her eyes that was immediately corrected with that weird smile.

This stunned Danny.

"Trying to move in on my girl, Espinoza?" Jason asked, laughing.

But Danny knew better. Guys only asked that if they felt threatened and didn't want to cause a scene. "Not at all. Just making sure Ella didn't dehydrate."

"I've been slacking on my boyfriend duties," Jason said, planting a kiss on her neck.

The look on Ella's face suggested she was enduring it and Danny turned away, uncomfortable by the public display of affection and Ella's odd behavior. He grabbed a few empty beer bottles and tossed them in the trashcan marked *bottles*. Then he grabbed what was left of his own beer and found another room to hang out in. He left the kitchen through another door and followed the voices of people until he stood on a back deck.

"Danny!"

His eyes turned toward the voice, and he immediately recognized Marie. With a smile, he nodded toward her and went to join her group of friends near the fire pit. They'd just put a new log on the fire and the flames whipped furiously in the large metal pit.

"You guys, this is Danny Espinoza." Marie gave him a pointed look. "Did you deal with your work thing?"

"They wanted me to come in. I told them I was hours away," he admitted. This made those around the fire chuckle.

"So, what's it like working security?" one of the guys asked.

He shrugged. "Lots of walking and telling people to pick up their trash. Kicking the homeless off of campus."

"I bet you have access to professor offices and stuff," he said.

Shit. Danny knew where this was going. "No. That's a different crew. I only work outside."

The guy's face fell. "Too bad."

"Hey, Danny?" It was Tyler.

Saved by my best friend, Danny thought. "Excuse me."

"Come back when you're done!" Marie called after him.

He gave Tyler a grateful smile. "You just saved me."

"From?"

"I think that girl has been flirting with me all night so she could introduce me to her friends who want to make a friend in the security business. For illegal means, I'm sure." Danny gave an exasperated eye roll.

Tyler laughed. "Well, you knew that was going to happen eventually."

He shrugged. "Yeah, I guess. What's up?"

"Hey, you're not really into Ella, are you?" Tyler winced.

"No."

"It's just that Jason saw you out on the front porch with her, then you got her a beer..."

Danny could tell Tyler was worried about his relationship with his roommate. "Jason has nothing to worry about. I have no interest in Ella. I was just being nice. I went outside to take a work call, and there she was. I asked her if she wanted another beer, end of story." *Besides, she gives me the willies,* he silently added.

"Great. Thanks," Tyler said, as if Danny had just done him

a big favor. And perhaps he had, if it meant no tension with his roommate. "So, what did work want?"

"What they always want. Someone to come in and cover an extra shift." Danny glanced down at the beer he'd been nursing for a half hour. It was warm now and still a quarter full. He dumped it into an empty planter by the back door.

"Well, I'm proud of you, man." Tyler patted him on the back.

"For?"

"For saying no." Then his attention turned toward whatever was going on inside the house. "Let's go back inside. Sounds like some crazy shit is going down."

Danny had no reason to stay out here unless he wanted to be accosted by students hoping to break into their professors' offices, so he followed. When they reached the living room, both he and Tyler's jaw dropped. On the heavy wooden coffee table was Ella, dancing and grinding against Jason while the onlookers hooted and hollered, some guys screaming out for her to *take it off*. It seemed Ella had become the life of the party.

"Maybe she is just awkward," he mumbled to Tyler. But deep in his gut, a sickly feeling nagged at him.

❧ 7 ❧

"Tyler is going to be so surprised," Ella said, holding the letterman jacket aloft for the shadows to behold before shoving it to the bottom of her backpack.

She'd been planning it for a few weeks now. The long drive to Ridgeway and back had been worth it. Her shadows helped make shorter work of digging up Bryson Day's grave. In the end, she'd gotten the letterman jacket off of the corpse, she'd stowed the corpse in a secret place where only she and her dark friends could find it, and she and the shadows had escaped the cemetery before sunrise. Now, the plan only required that she slipped the jacket into Tyler's closet when he wasn't home. The best part was, he wouldn't know it was her. He and Danny were clueless, though she'd been watching Danny. He wasn't a dumb young man, and while Tyler was smart, Danny seemed to recoil from her and watch himself when she was in the room. She didn't think he'd identified her yet. Of course, she had something special for him. While Tyler was her primary objective, Danny would be fun to play with. She let out a wistful sigh and glanced back down at the computer screen.

The anonymous email account had already been created, and she had finished writing the message. She re-read it and deleted the subject, changing it to: It's Getting Cold Outside. With a malicious grin, she clicked *save*. "I'll wait to send it until after I've put the jacket in his room. Then maybe I'll send messages every so often to keep him on his toes," she told the shadows. Again, they huddled in the sanctum of the dark hallway and wouldn't come out until sundown. The living room was far too bright. She closed the lid of the laptop, then turned toward the hallway. In her mind, she had a clear picture of the homeless woman who had yelled at her outside Jason and Tyler's dormitory. She didn't need another chance run-in with the homeless who could identify her. "Once the sun sets, I have a job for all of you."

"Yes?" one of them hissed from the murky depths of the hallway.

"Find the homeless woman. The one who lurks around campus. I think I'll have her for dinner tonight." Amelia, amused by her choice, drew in a deep breath and stood. "And I think I'll have some tea before I head to the university."

"Yes, Amelia," the shadows responded in unison.

It was amazing how easily she was making friends now. The alcohol helped her loosen up at parties, and since she'd started dating Jason, everyone knew Ella. It had been so easy to convince them she was one of them, even though deep inside, she hated the exhausting work of pretending. In the end, it would be worth it. She glanced at the clock. She only had one hour until her first class. Afterward, she would stop by Jason and Tyler's. If neither were home, she'd just use the key Jason had given her to get in. It hadn't taken much, really. Just a suggestive comment about turning up naked in his bed.

She had no doubt he'd already been telling everyone they were having sex. But if Jason was in, the trick would be getting him out of the room for a few minutes. Lifting an eyebrow, she realized she was going to have to work harder at seducing him for her entire plan to work. So far, she'd let him stay over a few times. She'd endured kissing and letting him put his hands all over her. As disgusting as it was, it was the only way for her to stay close to her prey. Ella's house was Jason's home away from home, and the excuse that her aunt was in Michigan worked on Jason, too. She'd had to throw him off the ideas of parties, though. Bringing attention to the house and letting just anyone in could inadvertently reveal that Betty was dead, and part of her was in the freezer in the basement, a snack for later. "Focus," she told herself. *It's all a means to an end, nothing more.* "Besides," her eyes settled on the backpack next to the front door. "I have a present to deliver."

The shadows cackled from the center of the house.

THE CAMPUS BUSTLED WITH STUDENTS RUNNING TO AND from classes, and Ella went through the tedious motions and played the part well. She'd even taken quizzes and turned in homework, none of it overtly difficult. Though it was growing tiresome, and she was wary of lingering in the mortal world any longer than she had to. She enjoyed the game - tormenting the living only to kill them in the end. Often, she spent lecture periods thinking of fresh ways to kill, each fantasy more horrific than the last. Each time, she imagined Tyler's fear and how that same fear would feed her, keeping her youthful for as long as she walked the Earth. Once she had taken her revenge and eliminated him, only then could she finally rest. Her mind went over the mistakes she'd made in Ridgeway. She'd been right to kill people Tyler knew. This time, however, she'd be more creative with the murders. All the while, no one would suspect sweet, innocent, popular Ella. When her classes were over, she headed over to Jason and Tyler's, her eyes searching the benches and near bushes and trees for the homeless woman who'd confronted her. Either the woman was now avoiding the university, or security had been doing a better job keeping the homeless off of campus. Hopefully the shadows could find her so Amelia could shut the woman's mouth once and for all. The last thing she needed was to be revealed before she had Tyler right where she wanted him.

She entered the dorm like she owned the place, waving at people she knew and saying *hi* as she went. Outside his door, she knocked, her heart thumping in her chest, hoping Tyler wasn't home. If neither were there, she'd be able to slip in and out in minutes. Jason answered in just a pair of jeans, no shirt. Putting on a big smile, she let her eyes slide over his chest. "Hey, handsome."

"Ell," he said, his eyes lighting up when he saw her. "Come in. We have about an hour before Tyler gets back." He bounced his eyebrows.

"In that case..." She let the sentence hang suggestively in the air between them. Then she sniffed him. He smelled like sweat.

"Just got back from the gym. I need to take a quick shower. Do you mind waiting?"

A crooked grin came over her lips. "No, I can wait. Hurry up, though. We don't want Tyler walking in. Now that I have a key, though, I can sneak in here before you get home, and you'll find me waiting for you in your bed."

He let out a nervous laugh. "With my luck, Tyler would come home early. Maybe you should give me a key to your place." Then there was a long pause. "About that key I gave you," Jason sounded sheepish. "My roommate wasn't too happy about that. So maybe me having a key to your place would be better."

A nervous knot formed in her stomach. "That would work great until my aunt got home and threw me out." She rolled her eyes. "At least here, if Tyler walked in, he would just back out of the room and leave. Also, it's not like I'm going to use your key unless you need me to grab something for you or you invite me to come over and wait for you in the room. In which case I'd hope you would tell Tyler about that plan, so he isn't caught unprepared."

"Good point," Jason grabbed a towel, gave her a quick kiss on the lips, then grabbed his shower caddy. "I'll talk to him about it. I'll be out in ten minutes. Make yourself *comfortable*."

Ella had no intention of making herself comfortable. The second he was locked away in the bathroom, she waited a few moments before wrestling the letterman jacket from the bottom of her backpack. She slipped over to the coat closet and gently opened the door. While she thought about hanging it up, she decided instead to shove it into the back behind a gym bag on the floor. She closed the closet just as quietly. Now she had to deal with Jason. She pulled her phone from her jacket pocket and waited. When the doorknob to the bathroom turned, she put the phone up to her ear and threw a mortified look onto her face. "No, Auntie. I'll do that right away."

The huge grin Jason wore began fading as he closed the door behind him.

"No. I don't mind at all. If not, I can pick it up and run it to FedEx. They're open until seven." She threw him an apologetic look. "Yeah, I'm leaving right now. I'll call you and let you know." Then she pretended to hang up.

"What's wrong?" Jason hurried to the bed and sat down beside her.

"I'm so sorry. It's my aunt. Apparently, she isn't feeling well and ran out of medicine in Michigan. She wants me to run home, get her spare bottle, and ship it to her." She stood.

"Can't the pharmacy out there just fill her prescription?"

"They did give her a few pills to get her through the next few days, but she's supposed to go to her doctor next month for a check-up, so no refills." She shrugged.

"I can go with you."

"No, I appreciate that, but my aunt doesn't really know I'm dating anyone, and I'd like to keep it that way. If you show up during the day, the neighbors will start gossiping about it. If that happens, she'll tell my parents and they'll be on my case. They're *super* religious." She gave him another apologetic look. "How about I make it up to you tomorrow night? Just you and me, maybe outside underneath the stars? A moonlit picnic?"

He let out a heavy sigh. "Okay. Fair enough." Then he kissed her again. "The things we do for family, right?"

"Yeah," she said with a giggle. "Thanks." Then she left, pausing at the door to blow him a kiss. She had to get home so she could send a very important email.

It didn't take long for the shadows to find the old woman. She was resting behind a dumpster in an ally next to an exhaust vent, where the warm air from the building's ventilation system made the chill October night more bearable. The shadows surrounded the aged woman as she clung to her backpack. "Who's there?" she called out into the din.

"Amelia, Amelia..." the shadows sang.

The old woman tried to get up, wanted to, but something kept her frozen against the brick and pavement. Fear. That was it. Ella could smell it a mile off. She pulled her folding knife from her pocket. It was time to have a little fun. "Ma'am? Are you okay?" she called down the dark passage.

"Who, who are you?" the transient asked, her ancient eyes trying to focus in the dark.

The shadows closed in just as Ella stepped around the dumpster, her eyes glinting with malevolence. "Do you know what time it is?"

Ella's dark friends cackled with glee.

The woman pressed her hands over her ears. "No. Shut up! Be quiet! I'm not listening. You're not real!"

With knife in hand, Ella knelt before the women, eyes fixed on her prey. She reached out and grabbed the old woman by her gray head of hair, lifting her from the ground with inhuman strength, and casually tossing her like a rag doll to the ground in the middle of the alley with a sick thud. Something snapped, and the woman cried out. But there was no one to hear her. No one to come to her rescue. It was too late at night and all had abandoned this part of the city except the vagrants and criminals, none of whom were about to step in.

Ella crawled onto the woman's chest, opening her mouth to reveal rows of razor-sharp teeth. A low growl emerged from her throat. The vagrant screamed, her eyes wide with terror and a hint of recognition as Ella slit the woman's throat to silence her. While she still thrashed about, Ella took the knife and cut out the woman's left eye, popping it into her mouth and eating it. The homeless woman seized, then went limp. Amelia removed and ate her other eyeball, enthralled with the sensation of it popping in her mouth when she bit down. She ate a few bites of the rancid, aging flesh before finally rising.

"Well," she told the shadows. "It's getting late. We should go home. Tomorrow is going to be a big day." She folded her knife and slipped it into her jacket pocket, making a mental note to wash it clean when they got home.

"Do we kill Tyler tomorrow?" one shadow asked impatiently. They kept trying to rush her, and she kept having to pull them back.

"No. Patience, my dear friends. There is plenty of time." They all slipped through the darkness unseen for several blocks, returning to Ella's car. She drove home, the shadows clustered in the back seat, a writhing demonic black mass of them.

"Then who do we kill tomorrow?"

She groaned. The shadows had such short memories. "It's the roommate tomorrow, remember?"

"Ahh...yes," they hissed in unison.

They probably had remembered; they just wanted her to kill Tyler faster. She sometimes wondered if they enjoyed torturing her victims as much as she did. With a heavy sigh, she turned on the car radio, the classical station, at low volume. They made it home without incident and slipped into the house unnoticed by the slumbering neighbors. Cleaning up from the night's kill had become routine, and Ella kept two sets of clothes for the occasion. It saved the constant need for replacing her wardrobe. The only drawback was she ran the washing machine every night. When she had cleaned up the knife, her clothes, and herself, she sat down for her nightly cup of tea.

It was time for the next part of the plan. A shiver of excitement ran through her and a genuine smile slipped onto her lips. She could finally eliminate her wicked, loud-mouthed "boyfriend" with the horrible shoes. Ridding the world of Jason Pensa would be her pleasure, and if all went right, she and Tyler would be closer than ever. "'Will you walk into my parlor?' said the spider to the fly," she giggled.

The shadows rumbled in response with thunderous laughter.

❧ 8 ❧

Tyler had originally planned for a quiet night in. The weather was getting colder in the evenings, with snow expected to pound the mountains and sprinkle flurries over downtown. He needed silence to tend to his fried brain after a brutal week of midterms. Even Jason had succumbed to the pressures of the week and lay on his bed, headphones on as he stared to the ceiling, completely zoned out.

Tyler became distracted, however, from the breaking news that had caught his attention while flipping through the channels. Rumors had been swirling around campus about a string of murders on the homeless in the area. Tyler had confirmed none of this, but the matter was now center stage, as a dead body had turned up on campus, just outside the aviation building where Tyler rarely walked past.

The initial reports claimed they had found a man, stripped of his clothes, his left leg shredded from the shin down. A dozen stab wounds peppered his chest and stomach, and they believed they'd found bite marks on the wounded leg, but would need to confirm after a closer examination by the coroner.

A graphic showed six men who had been murdered over the past two weeks, each one homeless, each killed in the middle of the night during sleep. Tyler closed the browser and leaned back in his seat, trying to grasp the reality that a serial killer was potentially roaming the campus.

Left one town of murder to arrive in the next, he thought, shaking his head. He expected a call from his mother later that evening once she saw the news, so sent her a quick message to let her know he was alright.

Tyler opened his school email to download notes he had sent to himself earlier in the day, but stopped upon seeing a new message from an unknown sender with a subject line of: It's Getting Cold Outside.

He frowned before clicking on it, expecting a spam message, but falling entranced as he started reading:

Hello Tyler,

It's cold out, don't you think? Maybe a nice jacket will keep you warm. I have just the one for you. It's in your closet. Have you heard of the dead people near your school? So scary what's happening... would be a shame if it never stopped. They never saw it coming, just like your friend. What was his name? Bryce? Something funny like that. Anywho, check out the jacket in your closet. Try it on for size. Should fit you just right!

See you later.

Tyler rubbed his forehead, trying to process what he had just read. It seemed a bit like a spam message that had maybe purged his computer for recently used words, but the email had no link. Spammers didn't just send out messages for the fun of it. If this was a genuine message, what was the sender's intent? To rattle him?

He went back to the beginning and read it again, trying to

get a feel for the sender's style. The only person who would know about Bryson, assuming that's who they incorrectly referenced as Bryce, was Danny. Bryson *and* the homeless murders. Not even Jason knew about Bryson, Tyler opting to keep that chapter of his life under tight wraps.

"Jacket in the closet?" Tyler whispered to himself, his eyes shooting to the coat closet that stood next to their front door. He knew of the two jackets he brought with him during the move and had seen three others that belonged to Jason. His stomach sunk at the thought of another jacket somehow being placed in there to correspond with the email. He nearly dismissed it as lunacy, but it had piqued his curiosity.

Tyler glanced over his shoulder to see if Jason was still in a daze and stood up on shaky legs. The thought of a surprise in the closet made his hands slick with sweat, his heart rate gradually increasing with each step he took. His eyes focused on the doorknob, as if he expected something from the other side to turn it and jump out. He had never really shaken the basic childhood fears that once plagued him, still lunging onto his bed at night to prevent his ankles from being grabbed by the monster that lived underneath.

When he reached the door, he continued to gaze at the knob, debating if he really wanted to let an email have this much power over him. Maybe Jason had learned about Bryson and thought it would be funny to pull a prank like this. While it wasn't comical by any means, Tyler hoped it was the truth. Anything else would only open the door to several more questions.

His hand wavered as he reached out for the knob. *Quit being a pussy, and open it already.*

He drew a deep breath and pulled open the door, letting the hinges creak as it swung in slow motion. The jackets he expected to see all hung from the rack, nothing extra slipped in between. Jason's gym bag lay on the floor, and that's where Tyler saw the new jacket, tucked behind the bag, smashed into the closet's corner.

He caught enough of a glimpse to make out the blue and white fabric, and seeing those two colors made his head spin. *No, it's not what you think. No way in hell.*

Fully committed to this endeavor, Tyler reached in and pulled out the jacket with no more hesitation. He gasped once it spread open to fully reveal itself as a letterman jacket from Ridgeway High School. The last name *Day* was on the back, causing Tyler to flinch and drop the jacket, the blood freezing in his veins as he stood over it with his mouth agape.

His arms started trembling as he reached into his pocket for his cell phone, needing to call Danny immediately. Jason heard the commotion and rolled off his bed to see what was going on.

"You okay?" he asked, his eyes studying the jacket on the floor before falling on Tyler's horrified face.

"Did you put this here?" Tyler demanded, pointing at it with a trembling finger. "Don't fuck with me and just tell me if you did."

Jason took a step back, eyes falling back to the jacket on the ground. "No, wasn't me, man—I swear."

Tyler heard a tinge of fear in Jason's voice, or perhaps confusion. But he didn't care, and instead immediately dialed Danny, his free hand nervously patting the side of his leg.

"Hello?"

"Danny, you need to get over here right now. . . something's happened."

"I'm working right—"

"I don't give a shit, this is an emergency. You can tell them I called it in."

"Dammit, Ty. Okay, I'll be there in three minutes."

They hung up and Tyler saw Jason had moved closer to

the jacket, crouching down to examine it for a closer look. "Don't touch it!" Tyler cried.

"Bro, you have to tell me what's going on," Jason said, standing up and crossing his arms, his momentary lapse into fear completely vanished.

"I don't know what's going on, but we have to leave that alone—it may be a piece of evidence."

"Excuse me?"

Tyler shook his head. "Not what you're thinking. This jacket belongs to my friend who was killed earlier this year—in my hometown. We recently found out his grave had been dug up. His killer was never caught, and we think she might come for me."

"Oh, hell no. You mean I'm in danger, too?"

Tyler shrugged. "Did you ever get that key back from Ella? I need to know, anyone who has access to this dorm is a suspect."

"Whoa, slow your roll," Jason said, his tone becoming defensive. "Careful who you're calling a suspect. I'm sure there's a logical explanation for this."

A knock came from the door and Tyler wasted no time dashing over to open it, letting Danny in. His eyes immediately fell to the jacket on the floor and he stepped around it, as if it were a dangerous animal that might snap at him.

"Okay, so this is really happening. Okay." Danny spoke in rapid spurts, his eyes bulging as he fought with himself to calm his emotions. His hand touched the pepper spray on his belt, and Jason took another step back.

"How is this possible?" Tyler asked. "It can't be the real jacket."

Danny shook his head. "It is. His grave is dug up, and now his jacket is here. She's back, Ty, and that's the truth we have to face head-on."

"What the hell are you guys talking about. I live in this dorm too, so I demand you tell me right now."

Tyler spun around. "Where is that spare key?! We need to know."

Jason opened his mouth and closed it, frowning. "I don't understand what that has to do with anything. Stop worrying about it already."

"It matters," Danny said, gaining some of his composure back, refusing to break eye contact with the jacket. "We need to know all possibilities that exist to get into this dorm. You guys lock the door every time you leave, right?"

"I do," Tyler said.

"You know I do," Jason added. "I have over $3,000 worth of shoes in here, you think I'm gonna take that chance?"

"So the door is locked when no one's here," Tyler said. "But that leaves the question as to the other spare key you gave Ella. We just need to know where it is. Make sure she still has it in her possession. If she lost it, or it was stolen, we have a big problem."

"Okay, I'll call her," Jason said and turned around without another word to dial his girlfriend.

"Does anyone else in the university have keys to dorm rooms?" Tyler asked.

Danny nodded. "I can look into anyone who does. I know the maintenance crew has a master key for all dorm rooms. I'm sure the school keeps their own spare copies for each dorm somewhere. I'll go right now and see what I can find. I'll call you."

Danny sprinted out of the room, hopping over the jacket as it continue to lay on the floor like a murder victim.

Jason hung up his cell phone and returned to Tyler. "She said she still has it."

Tyler shook his head. "It doesn't make sense. Someone

had to have access to get in here. Do you know anything about Ella's past? Where she's from? Who her friends are? Anything like that?"

"I know a couple of things. Look, man, we've only been dating a couple of months. She hasn't given me her life story. She's from Wyoming. Her family is really religious. She lives with her Aunt Betty who I've met and who is currently in Michigan looking after a sick friend. She has one close friend named Rachelle. You know her."

"Okay. But isn't it odd you don't know her parents' names?"

"I don't understand why I'm on trial here."

"So you don't know."

"She has nothing to do with this—she just has the fucking key. I told you that!"

"She may not have anything to do with this directly, but there is a link somewhere that is responsible for this jacket ending up in our closet. Look, I'm sorry if it seems like I'm overreacting, but me and Danny dealt with some serious shit back at home last spring."

"Just tell me."

Tyler paused and considered exactly how much he wanted to spill to Jason. He didn't think Ella would have done something like this, even if she had somehow found out about Bryson and his friendship to Tyler. She had been nothing but kind and welcoming to Tyler, despite her quirks. But the fact remained that Amelia Doss was back in action, and she had delivered this warning shot without being detected. Was Amelia actually capable of befriending someone in Ridgeway who had a connection to Ella—or Jason?

"A serial killer murdered multiple people in our town, including our best friend, Bryson Day." Jason glanced down to the jacket to confirm the matching last name stitched on it.

"He's the one whose grave was dug up yesterday. His corpse still hasn't been found, and now his jacket is here in our dorm. The killer was never caught, so we can only assume that she's the one pulling the strings."

"So why so many questions about me and Ella? We didn't even know about any of this."

"I know you have nothing to do with this, but I am concerned that you know nothing about Ella's past. Does she have any other friends that she talks about? Has she ever mentioned anything about Ridgeway?"

Jason shook his head. "No, she hasn't, and I don't know about friends outside of college. The only people she hangs out with are the same ones you have, at the parties."

Tyler scrunched his face and rubbed the side of his head. "Just be careful. Like I said, there's a link somewhere, and until we know what it is, you can never be too safe."

"Are you implying that my girlfriend has a secret serial killer friend, and that she's helping do her dirty work?"

"I'm not implying it, just saying it's a possibility."

Jason snorted and shook his head. "Listen to what you're saying, man. This is nonsense. I'm happy to help however I can, but you have to lay off these random accusations. I've basically been living with Ella for the last month, and trust me, there's nothing evil going on there."

Tyler nodded. "Okay. I'm sorry."

"I suggest you think things through before blurting out the first idea that pops into your head. That's a good way to lose a friend."

Jason grabbed his windbreaker and started for the door, also stepping over Bryson's letterman jacket.

"Where are you going?" Tyler asked.

"I can't be here. You need to get your thoughts together. I'm going to Ella's place. And don't worry – I'll call you if she tries to kill me."

He left and slammed the door behind him, earning a jolt from Tyler. He still had no interest in touching the jacket again, opting to sit down on his bed and stare out the window at the bustling campus, waiting for a call from Danny.

❦   *9*   ❦

Tonight was the night Jason Pensa would die. No longer would Ella have to pretend to be his girl-friend. Of course, this opened up another can of worms. It meant playing the grieving girlfriend and seeking out Tyler for comfort – an idea that made her stomach turn. But she was getting ahead of herself. *First things first,* she thought. As she got ready for their date, she hummed to herself. It was a familiar tune, but she couldn't quite place it. Humming another bar, she applied her mascara. Then it came to her. It was Mozart's "Funeral March". She finished getting ready, trying to shove the catchy tune from her mind. As she left, she took up the bag with all the things she'd been collecting to do what had to be done. Inside there was rope and an old bedsheet. In her pocket, her folding hunting knife.

Ella had taken to meeting Jason at his dorm. He'd asked if he could pick her up, but the last thing she wanted was people poking around the house, or anyone seeing him at her place the same day he died. She'd worked hard to keep nosy neighbors pacified, and her life beyond the college campus a mystery to everyone. There was no need to kick up suspicion by inviting people over. They could ask too many questions, or worse, find what little remained of Betty Mathers in the freezer, or her bones and remnants of flesh in the crawlspace. She didn't want to make the same mistake this time, so she'd been sure to eat as much of Betty as she could. She'd fed some of the woman's organs, and other inedible bits, to a neighbor's dog. It was mostly the stripped bare bones buried in the crawlspace now, and she left only a single calf and foot in the freezer. The stench of death still lingered down there, but she was pretty sure that was due to a raccoon or a cat having slipped into the crawlspace and died.

She was thinking about Betty's remains when Jason bounded down the stairs, his eyes alight with enthusiasm, and steps filled with youthful vigor. He pulled a set of keys from his pocket and waived them in the air.

"I'm driving," he said.

A pang of disappointment hit her stomach. It was probably for the best. He'd take her out for some vile meal, and she'd let him feel her up in the car before insisting they take a romantic moonlit walk with the promise of sex at the end. By then, campus would be mostly empty. She'd already mapped Danny Espinoza's beat and the timing of it all. The campus was decorated for the Halloween season, and all the trees had little fabric ghosts hanging in them. She'd chosen a remote path obscured from any cameras. The shadows disrupted cameras anyway, so that didn't worry her. She had hidden the bag behind the bench, next to the tree... She forced a smile. "Sounds great!"

Jason Pensa was five-foot-eleven, only four inches taller than Ella. Athletic with an average build, he had light brown spiky hair and blue eyes. Her eyes traveled down to his shoes. More than anything, she hated his shoes. Today's pair was white leather with a black logo on the side. "You like my Jumpmans?"

"They're awesome," she lied.

"I told Tyler that I was picking you up," he said.

Her face contorted with confusion. "Why? Is it wrong that I meet you here?"

"Well, it's just that my friends kind of think I've already met your aunt." He held up the key fob and the lights flashed on his black Honda CRV. "Will I ever meet her, or get that elusive key to your place?"

Ella paused on the passenger side while Jason got in. She shook her head in disgust and opened her own door and got in. This modern world was so rude and uncivilized. "I already told you she would have a fit if she knew I had a boyfriend."

"I just don't think all this sneaking around is good, you know?" He put his hand on her knee.

She put on the seatbelt, hating how the damn things always rubbed against the bottom of her neck. "It is when it's likely she would throw me out if she knew. I told you that my family is deeply religious. If I want to keep my room, which saves me a lot of money and keeps me from having to work, I have to wait until I graduate and have a job before I spring boyfriends on them." Then she gave him what she hoped was an apologetic smile. "Don't worry. I'll tell people you've met my auntie many times if you want me to."

That seemed to satisfy him for the time being. In the backseat, two of the shadows sat quietly. Jason didn't even realize they were there.

He took her to an inexpensive burger restaurant that also bore the decorations of Halloween, or *All Hallows Eve* as Ella knew it. Fake skeletons adorned the walls and rubber bats hung from the ceiling. She found it all rather curious. She never remembered All Hallows Eve being such a big deal in Ridgeway a lifetime ago. But this was also the big city almost a hundred years later. Things had certainly changed.

"Don't tell me your family doesn't celebrate Halloween…" Jason started once they'd sat and gotten their drinks.

"No. We didn't."

"What are your family then? Mormons or something?" He appeared genuinely perplexed.

"Something like that. I don't want to talk about them though." Not that there was much else to talk to him about, of course. Then their server showed up, and she ordered a burger, rare.

Jason cringed. "You really like it bloody?"

"You have no idea how good it is," she told him, trying hard not to laugh. "So why all the interesting shoes?"

He threw his head back and laughed. "We talked about this before. They're cool."

"Yes, so you've said. But why?" The weird shoes were really getting to her.

With a shrug, he leaned on the table with his forearms. Another annoying habit. "I like them. They're fashionable. Comfortable. They look good."

"Fair enough." It was her way of surrendering. She could let him have his shoe fetish for the last few hours of his life. It was the least she could do.

"Don't you have something you collect?"

"Thimbles," she admitted. When she was alive, she'd had an extensive collection of thimbles, though it seemed completely ridiculous now. "But they're not fashionable. I'm not upset I no longer have them with me, and in retrospect it was an odd thing to collect."

He chuckled. "What's a thimble?"

"They're for sewing, so you don't poke your finger while doing needlework." Then she realized how lame that sounded. "I thought I was going to be a clothing designer when I grew up." She didn't want him thinking she was too out of touch.

The answer seemed to work, but he clearly had no interest in thimbles or fashion design, unless it involved shoes. "So, what are we going to do after we eat?"

Her eyes lit up. "I had some ideas about that." *Men and their one-track minds. They're so predictable,* she thought.

"Oh?"

"I was thinking we could go for a moonlit walk on campus, maybe find a secluded spot..."

A lecherous smile slipped onto his lips. "And then?"

"Have you ever made love by moonlight?"

"Isn't it a bit cold?" He licked his lips.

"Not with your body on top of mine, it won't be," she said.

She expected he'd insist they leave right then, but he didn't. Instead, they finished their dinner, he paid the bill, and an hour later, they left.

He drove a bit faster on the way back to campus while he told her about all the concerts and sports games he'd attended. She merely pretended to listen. When they pulled back into the parking lot and he found a space, he shut off the ignition and just sat there for a minute. "Maybe we should just..." Then he leaned over and kissed her, and Jason Pensa turned into an octopus because his hands somehow found their way all over her body. Ella let him, cringing inwardly the entire time, but comforted by the knowledge that the end was in sight.

Jason pulled away for a breath, looking like he was about to make a suggestion. Ella placed one finger over his lips. "I have a surprise for you. I want you, but I want you under the moonlight, in a place where we could get caught."

A great big grin appeared on his lips. "Kinky."

"Come on," she whispered, slipping out of the car. Her eyes caught the shiny dome of a parking lot camera under one of the lamps, but she ignored it. The footage would only show up as a glitchy fuzz whenever she was around. The shadows always made sure of that. She started toward the spot and could hear Jason racing behind her to catch up, linking his arm in hers.

They hurried along the path, Jason revving, and Ella excited to finally be getting on with it. The shadows followed alongside, staying near the trees, their movements a macabre dance of death. The spot she'd chosen was rather remote—a quiet nook where students could relax and meditate in the small garden. Large maples, many of them still shedding their golden leaves, lined the path there. The frivolous ghost decorations hung in each of them. Really, they looked like nothing more than white sheets draped over balls or balloons.

Ella went straight over to the bushes, felt under them on the cold ground, and pulled out the bag. She took out the sheet and spread it over the ground.

Jason immediately sat down in the middle of it. "Well, I'll be damned, girl. You really thought this through."

"I wanted this to be memorable," she said, and she meant it.

"What else do you have in there?" He reached over to grab the bag.

She smacked his hand playfully. "Oh no. That's not for you. It's for me." She pulled out the rope.

"Damn, you really are kinky."

She pushed him back onto the ground, onto his back, and straddled him. "You have no idea how long I've been fantasizing about this. How bad I've wanted to do this." Then she leaned down and kissed him. She removed her blouse just as the shadows, hundreds of them, filled the small alcove, turning the entire area completely black.

Shoving her tongue deep into Jason's throat, she pushed her chest forward to meet his awkward hands and felt his growing arousal through his jeans. She rubbed herself against him, and before he even knew what was going on, she had the noose around his neck. Her teeth clamped down on his tongue and in one ripping motion, she bit half of it out and spit it onto the ground, just as she used her knife to sever his windpipe to keep him from screaming. All that came out when he tried to scream was a wheeze and some gurgling. The shadows went to work and hoisted him up and over a tree branch, his hands clutching uselessly at his neck, legs kicking frantically. Watching his struggle and bulging eyes grew tedious, so Amelia grabbed the end of the rope held by the shadows and gave it a swift yank with supernatural strength. There was a sickening snap, and Jason Pensa went limp. The front of his jeans a wet mess when he pissed himself.

Ella pointed to the sheet and whispered to the shadows, "Put that over him and make him look like the rest of the ghosts in this hanging graveyard." She wasn't hungry, so left him whole and intact.

"Yes, Amelia," they said. As if a light breeze had picked up the sheet, it rose and covered Jason's corpse and he did, indeed, match the rest of the ghosts. She put her blouse back on, then took the bag and slid it into the waistband of her jeans. She took the opposite path back to the parking lot where there were no working cameras, the shadows surrounding her as she went, obscuring her in darkness.

As she drove Betty's car home, she hummed Mozart's "Funeral March", again with a smile on her face. When the police showed up, she would merely tell them she and Jason went out for dinner, then he drove her home. He had, after all, told his friends that he was picking her up.

"What now?" one of the shadows asked from the backseat.

"We go home, and I practice being surprised, horrified, scared, and inconsolable with grief."

❧ 10 ❧

Danny had to work the late shift once again, but didn't mind at this time of year. Seeing the campus decorated for Halloween brought a special energy for his favorite holiday. The cold, foggy evenings put him in a productive mood to write his screenplay, and he had knocked out three more pages before stepping outside to make his last round across campus.

The colder nights kept foot traffic to a minimum, Danny alone in his thoughts for long stretches at a time. He still looked over his shoulder occasionally, half expecting Amelia Doss to show up one of these nights, but he had mostly put his paranoia to rest since they found Bryson's jacket. Danny had spent a solid six hours in the school's security system, sifting through virtual files of all persons with a way of entering a student's dorm room. He found eight total matches and dug deeper, browsing old records and social media accounts for anything that might tie them back to Ridgeway or Amelia.

After all that time, he came up with absolutely nothing, both frustrating and a relief. After double checking, Danny concluded it had to be Jason or Ella who had slipped the jacket inside. He discussed this matter with Tyler, who insisted neither had any way of knowing about Amelia or Bryson. But the connection was there somewhere, and he'd remain diligent in finding it.

For now, however, Danny enjoyed the decorations around campus, ghosts swaying from tree branches in every courtyard he passed, moving in the breeze with an eeriness that made him look multiple times to make sure he wasn't losing his mind.

He reached the point on the route furthest from the security office, the business school building that backed against Speer Boulevard and the rest of downtown Denver. Being closer to the city, Danny always had to check the narrow courtyard that separated the business building and a faculty office building, a common area for the homeless population to hideout for the night thanks its location away from security cameras and heavy lighting.

The benches were clear, and no one appeared under any of the trees. As the path led to a quiet nook, a lone ghost swayed from one of the branches of a lone tree, the only one present in this courtyard. He squinted as the ghost didn't quite look the same as the rest around campus. It didn't move with the same weightlessness as the others, twirling more than floating, and appeared slightly larger than the others.

Danny pulled out his flashlight and started into the courtyard, still keeping an eye for any homeless person attempting to hide in the shadows.

He stopped twenty feet away from the ghost. All the others hung from trees with fishing wire to give a true illusion of floating through the air. This one hung from a thick rope, the branch bending slightly as it resisted the weight pulling it down.

"What the fuck?" Danny whispered, scanning the figure

up and down, his heart stopping when he saw basketball shoes sticking out from the bottom of the draped sheet. "No."

His hands started shaking, the flashlight dancing around the hung ghost. He fumbled with his radio, accidentally smacking it as he tried to catch it, sending it tumbling toward the ghost. He refused to step any closer, opting to grab his cell phone and calling Tyler first.

"Ty, it's me. Is Jason there with you?"

He listened, eyes still glued on the figure.

"Okay, you need to come here immediately. I'm in the courtyard next to the business building. Hurry."

Danny hung up the call and dropped his cell phone back into his pocket. A disturbing reality had slipped into his mind that he was about to report a murder.

"It's just a prank," he assured himself. "It's that time of year."

While he enjoyed a good spook, the recent happenings with Byson made him jumpier than usual. He'd also fallen deep into the world of horror he was creating in his screenplay, so seeing something of this nature come to life before his eyes proved too overwhelming for him to process with logic.

"There's a dead body hanging from the tree," he said to himself, hoping the spoken words would somehow brace him for the inevitable truth waiting beneath that pale sheet.

Footsteps approached from behind, and he spun around, hand whipping to his baton. Tyler walked up to him, his steps heavy as he gasped for air after having run across the entire campus.

"What's wrong?" Tyler asked, his tone already braced for uncomfortable news.

"When's the last time you heard from Jason?"

Tyler looked around, but still hadn't noticed the hanging

ghost that differed from the rest. He shrugged. "I think he left our dorm around three . . . so five hours ago. Said he was going to Ella's place."

Danny nodded as if he expected this, then pointed his flashlight to the ghost, lowering it to reveal the shoes sticking out.

Tyler gasped and slapped his hands over his mouth. "No."

That was all the confirmation Danny needed. He had recognized the shoes—they were in immaculate shape. The pure white leather didn't need the flashlight to stick out, a black vinyl trim running along the bottom edge of the shoe, the familiar Jumpman logo stitched into the side.

"Are those Jason's shoes?" Danny asked, feeling it needed to be confirmed.

Tyler lowered his hands, eyes glued to the dangling shoes. "I mean, it looks like them. I'm fairly certain he has a pair that looks just like those. It could be someone else."

"I suppose—"

"Or it's a prank," Tyler interrupted. "Has to be. Now he's just fucking with me after everything with the jacket. I know I pissed him off by accusing Ella of being involved. He's just getting back at us, right?"

While Danny hadn't considered this, it was a possibility. One he hoped against all odds was true. He could handle a prank, but an actual death, not so much.

"I'm looking," Tyler said, stomping forward. "Not funny, Jason—you've gone too far." He reached the ghost and had a moment's hesitation before grabbing the bedsheet and pulling it upward. The feet dangled around his waist level, so he had an awkward angle to pull the sheet completely off. What he saw, however, was enough.

Tyler backed away, letting the sheet fall gracefully back down to cover the legs, and tripped over his own feet while walking backwards, eyes stuck on the ghostly figure. "Oh my

God," he muttered in a shaky voice. "It's him. It's fucking him."

Danny hurried to Tyler's side, reaching out a hand for his friend who had instantly become unbalanced as he crawled on the ground. "Ty, are you sure?"

Tyler nodded. "His eyes are open, his skin is white. Blood all over his shirt." He paused, gagging but not letting go of his dinner. "She's here, Dan. That bitch is back here . . . for us."

Danny had already been preparing for this possibility, assuming it a likely scenario after hearing about Bryson's grave. That was the warning shot she had meant to deliver, and it worked. If Amelia could only thrive when people believed in her, she had to do something drastic to get everyone thinking about her again. She found a way downtown, and Danny had to make sure no one else on campus learned of her story. If belief in her spread beyond him and Tyler, they'd have a nightly murder to clean up.

"You need to get out of here, and I need to call this in," Danny said, pulling out his cell phone.

Tyler regained enough composure to stand on his own feet. "Wait, what are you going to tell them? Have you even checked to make sure there's not something that will lead to us? What if she's trying to frame us for this?"

"You're already going to be questioned since you're his roommate. You and Ella will be the first two people the police want to speak with."

"Dammit," Tyler muttered, not having come to this realization on his own. "We just have to make sure Amelia isn't mentioned."

"No reason to mention her. We don't actually know that it was her, so no need to even suggest her name. As far as you know, Jason left your dorm to spend time with Ella—that should get the focus off of you."

"Okay. I'll go back to the dorm and try to act calm."

"Don't touch anything—especially if it belongs to Jason. They'll probably sweep your dorm tonight."

"Should we call Ella?"

"No. She'll be the primary suspect since she saw him last. Any communication to her now will only look suspicious. She's on her own for now—wait until they clear her name before talking to her."

"Okay, thanks." Tyler turned and hurried away, going back to his dorm where he'd surely lose his mind over the next couple of hours.

Danny called the police first, then followed up with a call to his manager to explain the situation. Both would arrive at the scene within the next five minutes. Until then, Danny wanted a look for himself, just to be sure that Tyler hadn't let his imagination get the best of him.

He looked around before proceeding, ensuring he was alone. He grabbed the sheet, surprised by its thickness, and raised it up as he crouched down for a better upward view. Jason's eyes indeed bulged, a look of sheer terror and petrification stuck on his face, suggesting his last moments had definitely caught him off guard. Dried blood oozed from his mouth, streaming down his throat and onto his gray shirt. The noose broke his neck, Jason's head cocked awkwardly to the side, a ring of purple lining the flesh just inside the noose.

"Jesus Christ," he whispered, stepping back and letting the sheet fall. He was convinced Amelia Doss had done this, but had no one to tell. If she was on campus, he and Tyler couldn't waste any more time tracking her down. Every day that passed from this point forward would remain ripe for a new murder to turn up. The police wouldn't have any chance of actually capturing her, especially since none of them would believe a wacky small-town tale.

Danny felt lightheaded and sat on the sole bench in the courtyard. His legs had grown weak, his mind flustered. He'd have loved to join Tyler back in his dorm and get to work right away, having to look for a whole new set of connections to explain how Amelia Doss ended up in downtown Denver. One matter gnawing at him was regarding how many people were talking about Amelia back in Ridgeway. Her legend lived on forever, but people like the sheriff and his deputy had witnessed her firsthand. Even if just those two had a private discussion after the incident with Bryson's grave, that might have been enough for Amelia to gain the strength and willpower to steal a car and learn how to drive it.

"Where are you?" he asked, looking around the campus. He felt confident in his ability to fight her again, but knew she would only be stronger than before. Amelia Doss was no dummy. She understood the mistakes she made during their last encounter, and would have spent the past several months dwelling on them, lusting for another chance to make things right. She needed more strength to finish the fight, and wouldn't be back unless she felt ready.

The time had come for her to make that next attempt, but one thing she couldn't account for: knowing Danny was equally ready for their showdown.

Tyler paced around his dorm after the police left. They had questioned him for an hour upon their arrival. Two detectives swept the dorm for clues who might have killed Jason, while another two officers asked Tyler questions about his time living with Jason, all the people he knew, and about their last interaction together.

They assured Tyler he was not a suspect, video surveillance around campus confirming that he had been in the dorm room during the time Jason was murdered. They had no leads at the moment, and were frustrated the cameras didn't cover the area where the murder had taken place and that other cameras, like the one in the parking lot, seemed to have intermittent interference.

They left shortly after midnight, at which point Danny arrived at the dorm, both of them unable to tease the prospect of sleep.

"What are we supposed to do?" Danny asked. "She's here, man." He paused and pointed out the window. "She's out there, probably watching us."

Tyler pulled out his cell phone and started dialing.

"Who are you calling?" Danny asked.

"Sheriff Abbott."

"It's the middle of the night!"

"He won't care."

Tyler waited as the phone kept ringing, about to hang up when a groggy voice finally answered. "Hello?"

"Sheriff Abbott, it's Tyler Reynolds. I'm here with Danny in my dorm room."

"Tyler? Do you know what time it is? I just went to bed a couple hours ago and have to be up at four o'clock."

Tyler heard the frustration clawing to the sheriff's surface, but his sleepiness dominated everything.

"I'm sorry, Sheriff, this can't wait. Someone was murdered on campus tonight and we believe Amelia did it."

"Hold on, let me get out of bed." Tyler waited as he listened to the ruffling of bedsheets and stomping around. "Okay, why do you think this was Amelia? No way she made it to Denver."

"We heard about Bryson—that had to be her. His letterman jacket ended up in my dorm closet. No idea how, no trace of anyone entering the room, but it's here. I put it back in the closet after examining it—it's definitely his. No one else would do that."

There was a long span of silence between them. "Christ," Sheriff Abbott said. "I've gone up to that old mine a couple times a week, just to see if I spot her in the area. Haven't seen anything, and we have leads on the Day boy's grave. Body hasn't been found, no evidence left behind."

"What about the people in Ridgeway—have they started talking about Amelia again?"

The sheriff chuckled. "Talking about her? People are obsessed with her story all over again. She's all anyone seems to talk about. All these unexplained murders, it's been bad. If it weren't for her, I'd probably be out of a job for not catching the killer. People accept she is somehow responsible for the murders. Not many speculate that she dug out that grave, but it doesn't really matter at this point."

"Sheriff, I know we told you how belief in her gives her strength. This is bad. She definitely gained enough strength to find her way to Denver. Shit!"

"Calm down, kid. Here's what we can do. You send me any news articles you come across regarding this murder on your campus. Once I have enough information that seems reasonable to grab my attention from Ridgeway, I'll call the Denver police department and chat with them about Amelia. I'll leave your name out of it, but will let them know we have a murderer who was never caught and had similar patterns to the murder in Denver."

"There's been more than this one. A bunch of homeless people have been killed in the middle of the night, right in the parks and alleys where they sleep. Stab wounds, bite marks, torn flesh. She may have been here longer than we thought. I'll email all the links I have on those murders—I've been keeping track of them."

"C'mon, Reynolds. Don't waste your college years trying to hunt a murderer. You should be studying and having the time of your life."

"Sheriff, if I'm not at least aware of what is happening, I may not have any more college years to enjoy. Me and Danny can never live freely if she is really out there."

"Fair enough. Just promise you two won't take matters into your own hands again. If she really is strong like you say, then you'll need more firepower."

"I'll do my best, and will be in touch. Thanks, Sheriff."

Tyler hung up and tossed his cell phone on his desk. "We're fucked. Sheriff said everyone in Ridgeway is talking about Amelia. All that belief in her . . . she has to be really strong now. What does that mean?"

Danny shook his head. "Let's not panic. Keep in mind, the strongest she might be is her regular human form. She won't become superhuman if even more people believe in her."

"That's supposed to comfort us?"

"We can fight a human woman, is all I'm saying. Now, this means she probably doesn't look like she did the first time. She *looked* like a zombie, but now will look more like a person: regular skin tone, clean hair. If she's been attacking homeless people, she might even be living among them. That's also a great way for her to stay off the grid."

"So she's definitely downtown then?"

Danny shrugged. "Most likely, but it's impossible for us know anything for sure. We really have to stay aware. We shouldn't go out alone at night anymore. Probably shouldn't go out alone, in general, but you'll be safer during the day when there are more people on campus. Don't go down any dark hallways or into empty rooms by yourself."

"Okay. How long do we need to do this?"

"Hopefully not long. I'm going to do some research about ways to send her back, or at least keep ourselves safe. I'll go do that now."

Danny started for the door, pulling out his baton and pepper spray, ready for any drama that might come his way once stepping outside. He reached the door, and Tyler stopped him.

"Do you ever think about that day? When you brought her back to life? What were we thinking?"

"I think about it every day. We were young and stupid. No point in dwelling on it now . . . I just have to fix it."

Danny offered a forced grin before opening the door and leaving the dorm, Tyler returning to his bed where he'd at least try to fall asleep.

He failed miserably, unable to erase the image of his dead

roommate dangling from the tree like a bunch of bananas. He looked across the room, the fancy shoes on display, and wondered whose job it would be to pack up Jason's things. Surely his parents would come out, but should Tyler help get a head start on packing? They certainly wouldn't be in the mood for such an activity. But it may have been improper for him to go through Jason's things without a blessing from the boy's parents. Everyone handled death differently, so he'd have to play it by ear.

A knock came on the door, pulling Tyler back out of bed as he assumed it was Danny returning already to share some interesting fact he had thought of during his walk out of the building. Instead, he swung open the door to see Ella, her hair a frazzled mess, black streaks running down from her puffy red eyes.

"Ella? What are you doing here?" Tyler asked, looking around the hallway behind her to see if anyone else had come. She stood alone, head hanging, eyes revealing the exhaustion they all felt.

"I'm sorry to be here so late," she said, sniffling her nose as her bottom lip quivered. "But I didn't know where else to go. After the police left, I couldn't be alone. Would you mind if I just came in and sat on Jason's bed?"

Tyler looked behind him as if the answer was waiting on the bed, but his true concern was how it might look to the police still investigating the murder, and likely keeping eyes on the two people closest to Jason at Denver State. Would they understand it was a matter of the victim's roommate and girlfriend grieving together, or would they jump to conclusions of their own?

He chalked it up as paranoia and stepped aside. "Come in."

Ella entered the room with slow, dragging strides. If Tyler

hadn't known any differently, he might have wondered if she had suffered a leg injury. "Thanks, Tyler."

She patted his shoulder before continuing to Jason's bed, first examining it like a foreign specimen, then sitting on the edge, planting her elbows into her thighs while her hands held up her head.

"How are you doing?" Tyler asked, taking a seat on his bed directly across from Ella.

"It's a weird feeling. Like we weren't lifelong soulmates, obviously, but it felt like we were on the verge of a really serious relationship. And just like that, it's over. We'll never know what could have been."

"I wish I could understand, but you're right—this is a unique situation."

"Yeah. Do I just start dating other guys again? Not saying I'm jumping back in tomorrow, but how much time is the norm for something like this? When the time comes, do I mention what happened to Jason?"

Tyler had no idea, and had never been one to give relationship advice. "I think when it's that time, you'll just have to trust your gut." He found it peculiar that this matter seemed to be Ella's biggest concern so close to Jason's death, but reminded himself, again, that everyone dealt with it in their own way. Ella's mind was surely processing millions of thoughts all night, and this is just where she was upon arriving at the dorm.

"Thank you. You were a good roommate... and friend. I don't know if Jason ever told you that, but he never had a bad thing to say about you."

This prompted Tyler to wonder if Jason had ever actually mentioned their fight over the dorm key to her. Surely he had nothing nice to say in the heat of the moment. There were also the accusations he made toward Ella, something that would have been impossible to keep to himself. He dismissed it and would bring up the matter at a later time—he still wanted that key back.

"That's good to know. I enjoyed living with Jason, too. I made some new friends thanks to him—ones I wouldn't have without him dragging me to parties . . . you included."

Ella grinned, tears still streaming down her face. "He loved to party. I'm really going to miss him. I can't believe he's actually gone."

The silent crying grew into heavy sobbing, Ella convulsing on the bed as she succumbed to the emotional pain of the night's events. She leaned even further down, her face nearly disappearing into her lap as all strength appeared to have left her body. Tyler stood up, unsure if he was supposed to physically console her, or keep spewing calming words that would only fall on deaf ears. He decided she was too far gone for kind words.

"It's going to be okay," he said, crossing the room and sitting next to her, the bedsprings groaning in protest at the added weight. He slowly, and reluctantly, slid his arm over her lowered shoulders, feeling the constant tremble from her body.

Tyler had so many questions he wanted to ask. What was the last thing she and Jason had done together? What was the timing of everything from when he had left her place and returned to campus? Had she spoken to the police yet, and if so, how did that conversation go? All of it would have to wait. For now, she was the wounded girlfriend grieving the sudden, tragic death of her boyfriend, and he was the only one there to comfort her.

Her crying didn't slow, the coconut scent from her shampoo mixing with the saltiness of her tears making Tyler nauseous. He ran his hand up and down her back, her spine bony to the touch, trying to will her to stop quivering.

"Everything will be alright," he whispered as they rocked slightly from side to side.

With her head so low, concealed by her dangling hair, Tyler had no chance of seeing the evil smirk plastered across Ella's face, left to believe that she was indeed mourning Jason's untimely death.

$\maltese$ 12 $\maltese$

Historical diatribes on witchcraft and necromancy were proving themselves worthless. Danny hadn't been able to find any easily workable spells or rituals to dispatch Amelia Doss, which made the library, despite its thousands of books, useless. One thing had become clear: Danny needed to find a legitimate source of odd ingredients and some sort of instructions. That was the only way they could get rid of Amelia for good.

Finding occult stores that specialized in witchcraft wasn't hard. A quick online search was all it took to find two of them within two miles of the campus, both a few blocks apart on Colfax Avenue, just east of the university. Danny only hoped that whoever was manning the shops had an extensive knowledge of necromancy and could guide him on how to lay to rest a disquiet spirit. He walked since the weather was still mild with the afternoon forecast predicting blue skies, a light breeze, and a balmy seventy-four degrees. As he strolled along, he silently rehearsed his inquiry, hoping he could leave some details out. After all, asking *how can I get rid of a deranged serial killer who has come back from the dead* sounded crazy, didn't it? With each step he took, his confidence waned.

He kept his eyes forward, ignoring the transients next to the buildings and the traffic buzzing by, wondering how many people in Denver Metro alone used magic for there to be so many metaphysical shops. *Metaphysical.* He began contemplating the word, his mind silently screaming, *but she's physical. There's nothing* meta *about her.* From his Dungeons and Dragons gaming days, he began going through the types of walking dead listed in the monster manuals. First, there were vampires. Vampires were undead and sucked the life from people via blood or psychic means. They also remained youthful. Amelia Doss didn't drink blood, but she certainly ate her victims and from what he'd seen, even though she appeared horrific when he last saw her, she didn't look entirely like the husk of someone once alive. Then there were zombies. They ate their victims, but usually a bite from a zombie turned the victim into a zombie, too. Next were the liches; often mages in life, they could move their souls from body to body, but eventually that vessel shriveled up and died. By contrast, Amelia wasn't shriveling up, and she didn't appear to have any magic other than whatever sorcery appeared to sustain her. She wasn't a mummy or a ghost. Mummies were, well, mummified. Ghosts didn't have physical form, or if they did - they appeared semi-opaque and could disappear. Then there were the banshees. Amelia didn't fit the characteristics of a banshee either. Of course, all of these creatures were fictional. Amelia Doss was anything but. So deep in thought, he almost passed the entrance to the first shop until he saw the candles in the window. Stopping abruptly, he turned back toward the entrance and looked up at the sign. *The Witch's Cauldron.* Drawing in a deep breath, he went to the door and opened it.

The cloying scent of incense wafted at him and assaulted

his senses, causing him to cringe. In the background, a sound-track of flutes drifted to his ears. The door closed behind him, the bell tinkling as it shut. Behind the counter was a balding, overweight man wearing jeans and a plain blue shirt. A lone woman browsed a bookshelf titled *Wicca*, and a gray tabby cat stretched out in leisure near the window, in a spot where the sun shone in. Danny looked around, not even knowing where to begin, so he chose the books. Chakras. Healing. Wicca. Candle magic. Astrology. None of the signage pointed to being the least bit helpful, so he moved to the counter. Behind the counter, on shelves that covered the wall stood jars of various herbs.

The man looked up from the book he was reading: *Everyday Astrology*. "Hi. Can I help you?"

This was it. "Do you have anything about getting rid of ghosts?"

The man's blue eyes gazed at him for a moment, almost as if he didn't understand the question. "Ghosts," he repeated.

"Yeah. I think my house is haunted," he lied. He glanced over his shoulder at the woman perusing books about Wicca, but she didn't turn around.

"What kind of activity?" the man asked. When Danny didn't immediately answer, he added, "Apparitions? Noises?"

How was he supposed to respond to that? He drew in another deep breath, unable to exhale the heavy scent of the incense. "Apparitions and things moving."

"I have just the thing," the man said. He came out from behind the counter and went over to the shelf holding rows of candles. Some of them in jars, others in the shape of humans. He grabbed something from the end of the shelf. "Have you ever done a smudging?"

"No."

The man held up what looked like a bunch of herbs bundled together with string. It was mildly shaped like a large joint. "This is a sage smudging stick. You light one end, and once it starts smoking, you blow the flame out. Then you wave it around until the smoke fills the entire room while commanding the spirit to leave your house. You do this in every room of the house."

Danny felt his brows furrow. "What about exorcism?"

The man laughed. "That can work if your belief system supports it, and a lot of cultures have exorcism rituals." He handed Danny the bundle of sage. "But it's been my experience that the sage works best."

Fighting back a sardonic smile, Danny took the sage. He could only imagine himself waving sage at Amelia Doss. She'd probably just laugh in his face, then stab him. "Anything stronger? What about to reverse necromancy?"

The man's eyes popped open wide, like saucers, and his expression turned grim. "Oh, that's heavy. We don't deal with that sort of thing here. That's black magic, and it's dangerous. You shouldn't mess with it."

Duly noted, he thought. Though it was a bit too late for that. It was Danny's foolish recitation of a spell that had brought Amelia back from the grave to begin with. Now, it was up to him to send her back. "How much for the sage?"

"Six dollars before tax," the man said.

With some reluctance, Danny paid for the rather expensive bundle of plants, tucked it into the inner pocket of his jacket, and left the shop, feeling the man's eyes on the back of his head as we went.

"Well, that was a waste," he mumbled under his breath as the door shut behind him. Back out on the sun-drenched sidewalk, he walked further up Colfax. It couldn't hurt to see what the second shop had. A dull thud pulsed behind his eyes and through his sinuses. It had to have been the incense.

The next shop, *Dark Works,* looked more promising from the outside. They draped the window displays with black cloth and there was a fake skull and black candles in one window. The other sported witchy-looking brooms, a stuffed black raven, and a few decorative knives. As he opened the door, he immediately felt a difference in atmosphere. Two women sat behind the counter, both dressed in black.

"Hello," the taller, raven-haired woman greeted. "Can we help you find something?"

Something about her tone put Danny at ease. "I hope so," he said, his eyes traveling around the shop, trying to take in just how much witchcraft paraphernalia was shoved into such a small space. It had a funny, distinct smell, almost like garlic and cloves. It wasn't too unpleasant, but at least it didn't appear they were currently burning any incense. "I'm actually looking to exorcise a malevolent spirit of the dead. It's something kind of like a vampire."

This piqued both women's interest. "There are a lot of different classes of vampire-type spirits," the shorter woman with brown hair said.

"I'm not sure what this spirit is exactly. I mean, I know she was alive at one time, then she died. Then she came back. She's violent. Evil." His words echoed through the shop. "She's retaken human form." He half expected them to call the cops to tell them a crazy man had come into their shop.

The women exchanged glances and the taller one raised an eyebrow. "It could be a demon."

"A...a demon?" He felt the blood drain from his face. While he never considered himself religious, the ramifications of the word demon struck fear at the core of his being. He'd never even considered the possibility that it was a demon who'd come back as Amelia Doss. Or that Amelia Doss had become a demon. "How would that work, exactly?"

"What do you mean?" the taller woman asked.

"How could someone who was a murderer in life come back as a demon?"

"Well, if this person had killed in life, their soul is tainted. They could become demonic in death, and not the good kind of demon," she clarified. "More like a devil."

"There's a good kind of demon?" He let out a nervous laugh.

"It's all in the semantics," she said as her co-worker, the shorter brown-haired woman, came around the counter and went over to a bookshelf marked *Evil Spirits*. "Some people believe demons are divine intelligences that are neither malevolent nor benevolent. Others believe there's nothing divine about them and that they're pure evil, hence—devils."

"So, I take it smudging with sage won't get rid of a devil?"

Both women laughed.

"Hardly," the taller woman said. "Devils require nothing more than a statement of intent to be summoned. Sometimes with blood, but not always. But because of that, getting rid of them, well, that can be trickier. Sometimes they're attached to an item or a person. Sometimes they're independent of a bond with anything on the physical plane. You'd almost have to know how the devil was summoned in order to get rid of it."

Danny thought back to the ritual they'd done. That was all he'd done – released a statement of intent - and that had been enough to raise Amelia from the dead. According to the woman, then a similar ritual, in reverse, should easily send Amelia back. *Jackpot*, he thought.

The tall woman went on. "Devils can have vampire-like tendencies. Sucking the life from those around them. Some people even believe that they can be summoned by one's mere belief in them."

He stood, frozen to his spot, and the shorter woman returned to her place behind the counter with two books. She lifted the books and waved them at him. "These two books should help. They're about how to protect yourself from evil spirits and send them back from whence they came."

"Will I need other supplies?" He willed his legs to carry him to the counter, and his eyes went down to the books sitting there. One was titled: *The Guidebook of Evil Spirits*. The other was: *The Grimoire of Malevolent Spirits*. Both books by the same author, E. F. Black.

"Well, since it takes intent to raise a malevolent spirit, that's usually all it takes to send them back," the taller one said. Then she lifted a slim, perfectly manicured finger with a silver ring on it. "But you might want something for protection. If you know the spirit's name, you can sometimes have power over it. But not always. That's why devils are so tricky. There doesn't seem to be a single thing that rules them all." She peered into the display case that made up the counter, then bent down and reached in, taking out a leather corded necklace with a single black stone. "Black tourmaline. It protects against evil spirits and keeps them from attaching to you." She handed the necklace over to him and he ran his fingers over the smooth stone.

"Do you think this will really work against a devil?" he asked, wondering if he should get one for Tyler. At twenty bucks each, he decided against it. It was doubtful Tyler would wear one anyway, but it didn't hurt to have one, just in case.

The short one shrugged. "Witches have sworn by black tourmaline for protection for centuries."

That didn't ease his mind, but he was willing to try anything at this point. Anything to keep Amelia Doss at bay. Denver's homeless population, on the other hand, wouldn't be so lucky.

"Of course, if you have any questions..." the tall one handed him a card.

"Thanks," Danny said, wondering if a simple necklace could keep him safe from the likes of Amelia Doss. While he still didn't have all the answers he wanted, at least he'd gotten something more than a bundle of herbs from this store. He paid for the purchases, bade the witches of Dark Works goodbye, and headed back into the bright afternoon feeling a bit more confident. While he was certain he'd have a lot more questions, he wanted to read the books first. The card they'd given him had both a phone number and email address. It made him feel a little safer knowing he had a couple of obviously knowledgeable twenty-first century witches he could contact if things went sideways.

❧ 13 ❧

So far, Tyler hadn't asked Ella about her last night with Jason, and she didn't mind.

The memory was so vivid. The detectives had come to the house early in the morning the night Jason died, and Ella had been waiting for them in her pajamas. When they told her what happened, she fell to her knees and wailed. It helped bring actual tears to her eyes when she thought about her own death and how painful it had been. But the police had bought her story. Yes, she'd gone out to dinner with him, but he'd dropped her home before going back to campus. There was no camera footage of Jason at all.

"We should probably scratch her off the suspect list," she'd overheard one detective say when she excused herself to use the bathroom.

"Mmmhmm," said the other. Once she returned to the dining room table, they stood. "We're very sorry for your loss, Miss Jones."

Ella sniffed, nodded, and produced a few more tears. "Thank you." She led them to the door, and they left. Once she'd locked the door behind them, the tears stopped, and she sat in the house's silence staring into nothing.

"Amelia?" one of the shadows had asked.

"What?" She remembered that the shadows had been kind enough to stay out of sight while the detectives where there, but they'd returned the second the house was empty again.

"Do we get to kill Tyler soon?" one of them cackled with glee.

"Soon," she'd said with an absent wave of her hand. "First, I need to see if I can keep crying at the drop of a hat. I'm not sure I possess enough grief, not even over my own death."

The shadows sighed and heaved around her, breathing in their own darkness.

Rachelle had been annoying, showing up at Ella's unannounced that same morning and letting her know that she'd probably get a pass in all of her classes for the semester since her boyfriend had died. Ella had produced more tears, drawing sympathy from Rachelle. But Ella hadn't wanted Rachelle's sympathy. She wanted Tyler's. How else could she get close to him?

Now, for second time in a week, she stood outside Tyler's dorm room door, her hand poised, ready to knock when the door opened. There was Tyler, carrying a book bag. "Ella!" He sounded surprised to see her.

She gave him a sad smile. "Hi. I just thought I'd stop by to see if you wanted to have coffee or something."

He pulled his phone out of his pocket and glanced at it. "Well, I was planning to go to the library for a while to do some research for a paper..." Then he paused. "But a quick coffee would be okay."

A spark of hope flickered inside her. Perhaps he really was warming up to her? "Great, thanks. I guess I just need to be around someone who knew him, you know? Does that sound stupid?"

"No. Not at all." He put his hand on the small of her back, ushering her back through the hall and down the stairs. "How are you doing?"

"As well as expected, I guess." She gave him a small shrug. "It's been rough with my aunt being in Michigan."

"Your aunt is in Michigan?"

"Yeah, sick friend. Cancer."

"That's rough." Tyler seemed uncomfortable.

"Did Jason ever tell you how crazy religious my family is?" she asked. She needed to draw Tyler in. Make him see the Ella she'd created as a real person with a backstory because then she'd seem like less of a threat.

"No, he didn't. Crazy how?"

She let out a weak laugh. "Like they didn't want me to go to college in the first place and told me I couldn't have a boyfriend."

His eyes widened in surprise. "Yikes."

"Yeah. It was only because Aunt Betty told them she'd keep me out of trouble and make sure I could live with her that they let me come all the way from Wyoming." They walked toward the coffee bar, careful to avoid the pathway along which Jason had died.

This seemed to pique Tyler's interest. "Have you always lived in Wyoming?"

"Yeah. Archer, Wyoming. Just a few miles east of Cheyenne." Ella had done a little homework in order to make her story sound more convincing.

"So why Denver State?"

She laughed again as they ambled along. "Because it was an entire state away. Don't get me wrong. My parents are decent people, but they're a bit old school. For example, thinking I shouldn't date until I'm out of college."

"Surely they know you're going to date," he said.

"Probably. I don't know, my parents are just weird. Smothering, almost." She wrapped her arms closer to her chest. "What about you? Does your family live around here?"

He gave her a strange look. "I come from Ridgeway, Colorado."

Ella made sure to furrow her brow. "Where's that?"

"Up in the mountains. It's a small town," he clarified, seeming to breathe a sigh of relief. "No one's heard of it."

She threw him a wry smile. "No one knows where Archer is, either. Looks like we're both just a couple of small-town kids who moved to a city." She looked over toward the towering buildings of downtown Denver. "I imagine this is smaller than places like Chicago and New York, but for me, it might as well be."

Tyler nodded as if to agree. "What's your poison?"

"Mocha latte?"

"Let me get it." He set his book bag on a bench and ran to the walk-up order window, giving Ella no time to refuse his offer.

Sometimes, when she got into character, Amelia briefly forgot who she was and really related to Ella. She was kind of enjoying the part more and more. She'd never been popular in her own time. She was never a social butterfly. Ella, on the other hand, was popular and had more friends than Amelia Doss ever could imagine. In that small way, being Ella was gratifying.

Tyler returned with two coffees and handed her one marked *mocha*. "Thanks," she said.

"Being in a big city, have you ever thought of serial killers?" he asked out of the blue.

Her eyes popped open with genuine surprise. "I haven't given it any thought. Why?" Her jaw dropped, another carefully chosen reaction. "You don't think Jason..."

"I don't know. You've heard about the *Homeless Killer* going around though, haven't you?" He cringed slightly.

"That's horrifying. I don't even want to..." She pretended to be upset rather convincingly.

"Sorry. I know, it's too soon. I shouldn't have brought it up. I didn't mean to upset you."

She swallowed hard, but mostly to keep from smiling. "No, it's okay." She let out a quick sigh. "I don't even like horror films or crime shows."

For a brief minute, they stood there, sipping their coffee, neither of them saying anything. "I should get to this paper," he finally said, his voice apologetic.

"Yeah, I have to meet up with my friend Rachelle before our American Lit class." They both parted ways when Ella had a brilliant idea. She whirled around and called after him, "Maybe we can hang out, have lunch or dinner sometime this week?"

Tyler paused and turned back toward her. "Yeah, sure."

"Great. See you later!"

"All right. See you." Then Tyler turned back toward the library, and Ella breathed a sigh of relief.

She pulled her phone from her pocket, checked the time, then made her way toward the courtyard where she often met Rachelle for their pre-lit class chats.

The entire time Rachelle was yammering on about classes and some guy in her philosophy class she was into, Ella just nodded and smiled, only half listening. Instead, her mind was categorizing all of the different ways she could terrorize Tyler and those around him. Earlier in the day, when she and Tyler had been talking, the idea to make lunch for the students had come to her. She smiled and glanced at her watch, then gave Rachelle an apologetic look. "Looks like it's time for classes."

Her friend stopped talking, nodded, and picked up her backpack. They walked to class together.

She finished out her day at the university, then put her plan into action. The cafeteria. That's where she needed to be. When she arrived, she got herself a drink and then found herself a quiet corner table, pretending to work while the dinner hour came and went, and the cafeteria started dying down. She glanced at her phone. It was nine o'clock. She'd spent most of the time looking up recipes for hamburgers. Back in her old life, she'd loved to cook for others. There was nothing like the validation from a meal well received.

It seemed most modern students liked hamburgers, including Tyler and his friend, Danny. She'd seen them eat enough of them to know that at least one of them would be enticed. She also knew that her burgers would be the talk of the campus if she did it right. All she needed was some onion, breadcrumbs, salt, pepper, spices, and a few eggs. The meat, of course, would hopefully have a higher fat content than the lean ground beef the cafeteria usually used. Fighting back a giggle, she put everything back into her bag, then slipped from the corner table into the bathroom while the people working the kitchen started cleaning up. All she needed was meat.

When the clanking stopped and the cafeteria went quiet, she slipped out of the bathroom, knowing that eventually, a janitor would be by to clean the toilets. The lights had been dimmed considerably, and from the kitchen, she heard a lone woman singing, running water, and a pan clanking. There was a straggler. A sly smile slid onto Amelia's lips. She wouldn't have to go out and hunt for meat after all. Nor would she have to wait for a janitor.

Slipping into the kitchen was remarkably easy. She stowed her backpack in a cupboard and took off her jacket and blouse, leaving them with the backpack. Now dressed only in a black cami and black jeans, she could get a little messy, cleanup would be easy, and no one would see the blood if her clothes got splattered. She took the folding hunting knife from her pocket and opened it, creeping up behind the short, thick older woman who the students knew as Mrs. Casey and referred to affectionately as Shannon. In one swift motion, she brought the knife around the woman's neck and slit the trachea and the jugular, then pushed the thrashing woman forward into the large industrial sink. The pan she'd been rinsing clanked to the bottom of the sink. The running water muffled the sounds of the struggle as Ella held the woman steadfast until her thrashing grew weaker, and her blood spurted from her neck with each heartbeat and rinsed down the drain with the water. When Mrs. Casey stopped moving, Ella lifted the body up, propping the woman's legs against the cabinets. It was best to drain a freshly slaughtered animal upside down.

Her eyes searched the kitchen for the tools she would need. The cafeteria certainly wasn't a slaughterhouse and had nothing to break bone or grind up entrails. She did, however, find knives sharp enough to carve raw meat and skin an animal. The rest of Mrs. Casey would have to be wrapped up and put in the freezer. Ella got to work, pulling out all the spices and breadcrumbs she'd need. She found the meat grinder, and a large bucket of already ground beef. She'd mix it half and half just to save time and keep from getting caught. Glancing at the body still draining in the sink, she tried to guess how many pounds of meat she'd get from the glutes and thighs. She might have enough to only mix up one bucket. She found some onions as well. Then she went to work undressing the corpse and washing its skin to make sure the meat was clean and fresh. She carved the pieces directly from the carcass, removing almost ten whole pounds from the buttocks and thighs.

When she finished, she took plastic wrap and some burlap cloth she'd found to wrap up the rest of the body before heaving it into a dark corner, behind some shelves in the walk-in freezer. Returning to the kitchen, she peeled off the skin, didn't bother trimming the fat, and then ran the meat through the meat grinder. She added this to the already ground burger, along with the spices, breadcrumb, a few eggs, and some diced onions, then put the bucket of meat for tomorrow's burgers back in the refrigerator. Finally, she cleaned up the kitchen, rinsed out the sink, and began washing the floor.

"Late night, Shannon?" a man called from the dining area of the cafeteria.

"Yeah," she called back, realizing she'd finished just in time. "Almost done. Just had to finish cleaning the pots."

"All right. You going to slip out the front or the back?" the man asked. She guessed it was probably the janitor.

"Probably the back," she said, staying behind the rows of bread carts so he couldn't catch a good glimpse of her, or recognize that her voice differed from Mrs. Casey's. She was counting on him not noticing.

"Damn messy kids. They're practically adults, and you'd think they never ate at a table before," he said.

She laughed and turned out all but the lights marked *leave on at night*. "Well, food falls, you know? Otherwise, I wouldn't have to mop up back here."

"Fair point."

"Well, I'm off. See you tomorrow night." She grabbed her blouse, jacket, and bag.

"Later, Shannon," the man said.

Ella slipped out the back door, adrenaline racing through her veins, and practically skipped to her car. She'd forgotten how much she enjoyed working in the kitchen and making meals for people. She just knew her fellow students were going to love her and Shannon's burgers.

❃ 14 ❃

Tyler waited outside the security office, Danny soon to be off his shift in time for them to grab lunch together. They'd been texting back and forth the past couple of days, trying to figure out a plan for the next steps they needed to take. A detective had stopped by one last time to sweep the dorm for any hints at who might have wanted Jason dead. Shortly after they left, Jason's older sister came to collect all the belongings left behind, tearfully packing up the half of their dorm within two hours, leaving nothing behind but a bag of trash.

Tyler had briefly considered requesting a move to a new dorm, the thought of living in a half-empty unit somewhat disturbing. But after more consideration, he decided to stay and gradually expand his belongings across the entire dorm since the university had informed him the logistics would be too strenuous for the middle of the semester. He had offered Danny to stay over whenever he wanted, but his friend always declined because of the scarred images he'd forever have of being the first person to come across Jason's hanging corpse.

Danny strolled out of the security building, backpack

slung over one shoulder, a solid black baseball cap low over his brow. "Hey," he said softly. "Ready for lunch?"

Tyler knew whenever Danny fell into a pit of research, whether for school or pleasure, he always seemed to be in a sulking mood. This instance was no different. "I've been ready all day. So looking forward to having a somewhat regular day. Had my morning business class—bored me to death. Had trig right after, and that was even more of a snooze fest, and now I get to have some Denver State slop to wash it all down. Like I said—a normal day."

Tyler thought he might have tried too hard until Danny cracked a slight grin. "Yeah, and I spent the morning doing homework for British Literature—just as riveting!"

They shared a laugh and started walking away from the security building. "So what's the word in the security department?" Tyler asked. "I'm sure you guys have heard more about Jason than anyone else."

"You'd be surprised—not much is shared with us. Once the police take over, we're left out. I, however, have had the great pleasure of telling the story at least fifteen times to everyone who works in the department. They just want to hear about it. I've become somewhat of a celebrity in the security building . . . kind of annoying."

Tyler chuckled, knowing such a fact would indeed bother Danny. He hated attention, so having all of it for the next couple of weeks surely contributed to his sour mood. They reached the Tivoli building that housed the student union and food court, and entered to a mob of students gathered on their lunch break. The odors of pizza and French fries filled the air, the elevated chatter making it impossible for them to hear each other as lines spilled out from the seven different food stations on the main level.

"I'm feeling a burger today," Danny said, starting toward

the hamburger stand without waiting for any agreement from Tyler.

Guess we're having burgers, Tyler thought, jogging to keep up. The burger line looked to be the shortest, surely appealing to Danny's disdain toward standing around and doing nothing. "Just be glad the whole school doesn't know you were the one who found Jason. This entire building would come up to you to talk right now."

Danny smirked. "And I'd tell them where to stick their request to hear the story for the eleven millionth time. I've already moved on, just wish everyone else could."

While he may have pushed aside the fact that he had found Jason dangling from the tree like a stuffed piñata, Tyler knew Danny was far from moving on. The work was only beginning behind the scenes.

Tyler looked around the room, spotting Ella at a table with a group of girlfriends. She waved at him to come over, and he replied with a thumbs up before turning back to Danny.

"Really?" Danny asked. "I thought you and I were going to have lunch?"

"We'll just say hello then go find our own spot. I'm sure she's leaving soon, anyway."

Danny rolled his eyes. "I don't see what the big deal is about Ella. Sure, she's attractive, but there are plenty of hot girls around campus. Nothing special about her."

"Just being nice, Dan. She's going through a lot right now. I'm just being a friend to her since Jason died."

"If you say so."

"What is that supposed to mean?"

Danny shook his head and stepped up to the counter to order his lunch, Tyler begrudgingly following behind as he asked for his double cheeseburger with a side of fries. Within a minute their food was placed on trays and the two swiped their student IDs to pay, Danny dragging his feet in Ella's direction.

Tyler again had to jog to keep up. "Danny, seriously, just a quick hello."

"I'll believe it when I see it."

Tyler continued ahead, growing annoyed by Danny's snappiness. Ella stood up with a warm smile, looking more relaxed and rested compared to the day before when she'd showed up at his dorm room and they'd grabbed a quick coffee. The bags and redness had left her eyes, and her hair gleamed shiny and silky.

"Hey, Tyler! Hey, Danny!" she greeted, stepping back from the table to give Tyler a quick hug. She did the same for Danny, who stubbornly kept both hands on his tray and turned his body sideways. Tyler couldn't help but let out a soft chuckle, wondering why his friend harbored so much disgust for Ella.

"How have you been?" Tyler asked.

"I'm in a much better place today. Still been a lot to process, but I'm no longer crying myself to sleep every night. Taking it one day at a time, you know?"

"I'm so glad to hear that. It's been weird in the dorm now that it's all cleaned out, but I'm gonna turn it into a mega room for myself."

Ella giggled and slapped Tyler on the arm. "You're too funny. I'll come keep you company if you're ever lonely."

Tyler's palms moistened and the tray in his grip felt like it could jump right out and spill on the floor. "Sure, I'll let you know. Well, me and Danny are gonna go eat. We'll talk soon."

"Don't be silly, you can sit here with us." Ella waved her arm and showed them the two open seats across the table. The three other girls all stared at Danny and Tyler, trying to get a read on them.

Tyler looked back to Danny who had a smug grin plastered across his face, his eyebrows raised to say *I told you so*. Back in middle school, they could have probably carried out this entire discussion through the simple movements of their eyes, but Danny had since become too reserved to allow such a thing anymore.

"Okay, thank you," Tyler said, shuffling around the table to the open chairs. Danny followed, dropping his tray on the table with attitude, his silverware jingling together. "You eat anything yet?" Tyler asked, hoping to keep the conversation light and steered clear of Jason.

"No, I haven't decided what I want. You'll have to tell me if the burgers are any good. They smell *awesome*." She smirked as she looked down at the table where a notebook lay splayed open. Ella realized Tyler saw the notebook and promptly slammed it shut, earning a giggle from the other girls around the table.

Tyler felt like he was back in high school thanks to their immaturity. He picked up his burger and sunk his teeth into it, the flavors from the ketchup and onions bursting over his tastebuds. The meat was softer than he expected, tearing away with the ease of ribs that had been slow-cooked for twenty-four hours. The sweetness of the meat made him look at the burger, making sure they hadn't mistakenly served him pulled pork. It was a solid patty, and he took a second bite to make sure he wasn't losing his mind.

"Something wrong?" Danny asked, seeing Tyler's scrunched and confused expression.

Tyler shook his head and dropped the burger back on his tray. "Just tastes a little weird. Like if the meat was cooked next to something else. I'm getting the flavor from whatever that was."

"Oh? You should take it back and tell them."

Tyler looked over to the line, which had doubled in size.

"Ugh, I'm fine. I'll try to take a couple more bites and call it a meal."

"Suit yourself," Danny replied with a dismissive shrug, shoving his own burger into his mouth without a second thought. "I see what you mean. It's a little sweeter than usual, but not bad." He took his next bite as if proving his point.

"So how are your classes going this semester?" Tyler asked, again returning to small talk.

"They've been okay. School is school, right?" Ella replied.

The other girls snickered around her, like trained robots programmed to make her seem funny.

"The dean offered to pass me for all my classes this semester," Tyler said. Danny dropped his burger and looked up from the trance he had fallen into.

"What?!" Danny gasped. "Are you shitting me?"

Tyler nodded. "I declined. He said it was a unique situation, having my roommate pass away in the middle of the semester. And since all of my classes are mostly a repeat of my last year of high school, he'd have no issue letting me take the semester off."

"You turned *that* down?" Ella asked, puzzlement washing over her face.

Tyler shrugged. "I honestly enjoy school. No idea what I would do with all that free time. Would probably sit in my dorm and go crazy, and I'm sure that's the opposite of what the dean was hoping to accomplish with his offer."

"Jesus, Ty, you're nuts," Danny said. "I like school, too, but damn, you gotta know a good offer when it's dropped in your lap."

"Enough about the offer, I'm happy with how things are."

"That's very admirable of you, Tyler," Ella said, grinning across the table. "Says a lot about you as a person."

"Honesty is soooo important," the girl next to Ella added, smirking as she refused to break eye contact with Tyler.

He wondered who exactly these girls were, having seen none of them at the parties he used to attend with Jason. They seemed an odd bunch to form a posse around Ella, but he supposed she could have gravitated to the first people to be kind after the tragic loss of her boyfriend. It wasn't the first time someone had made a bad judgment call in the wake of emotional distress, and Tyler wondered if he had made the same mistake by not taking the free pass for the rest of the semester.

Tyler took another bite and forced it down, shaking his head. "Sorry, I can't do this. You want the rest, Ella?"

Her face lit up, unable to hide her gratitude for the simple gesture. She nodded and Tyler pushed the tray across the table where Ella snatched up the burger and took an aggressive first bite.

"Tastes fine to me," she said between bites.

Tyler leaned back and watched her eat, noticing for the first time the gentle sparkle in her eyes, the small dimples that formed at the corners of her mouth whenever she smiled. His stomach churned with a distant, yet familiar, sensation. He felt his heart drumming a little faster beneath his rib cage, the room spinning around him as the thought of kissing Ella rushed into his thoughts.

Slow down, he thought. *It's way too soon to fall for her, and probably* completely *inappropriate.*

Tyler shook his head free of the thoughts, knowing a girl of Ella's caliber would never fall for a nerdy kid from a small mountain town. There was a reason she and Jason hit it off in the first place, and it wasn't because Jason wanted to stay home on Friday nights to watch a documentary on the Persian Wars. Despite his resistance, Tyler watched Ella finish the burger, and couldn't help but admire a girl who could eat.

15

Since Danny had the rest of the day off and had finished his homework for the day, he and Tyler spent the afternoon in Danny's dorm room. His parents had paid extra to ensure he'd have a place to himself, no distractions of a roommate to keep him off course from his studies. Danny didn't care, knowing if he had a roommate, he'd have ignored them just the same to get work done, especially once it came time to write his screenplay.

They entered the dorm, and Danny tossed his backpack on the foot of his bed. He didn't bother with decorations, his walls bare except for a calendar hanging above his desk. The desk itself was incredibly organized, the space clear except for a laptop and wireless mouse. Even the keyboard was tucked into a slide-out drawer below, out of sight. A framed picture of Danny with his parents stood on the back corner of the desk, his Ridgeway High School tassel dangled over the corner.

What he wanted to talk about was the occult research he'd conducted so far. To tell Tyler about his visit to the strange stores. What came out of his mouth instead was: "So are you falling for Ella now that she's available?" He sat down heavily at the foot of his bed.

The single resident units were slightly smaller and came furnished with a small sofa. Tyler sat on the couch and leaned back into the thick cushioned armrest. "Falling for her? No. But there is something about her I can't quite pinpoint. Like... I want to get to know her better. She's always been a sort of mystery, and even after the time we all spent together, she kept to herself or to Jason."

"I don't know, man. I get that she's attractive, but I've never been impressed by her personality. Seems kind of shallow to me. And are you sure you'd even want to go down that route? It sounds like she and Jason had sex all the time. No offense, but she might be a bit too much to handle for a virgin like yourself."

Tyler grinned, and Danny knew he had got him. They always teased each other about their virginity heading into college, vowing to lose it their freshman year. There had been no golden opportunities yet, but the semester was only halfway over. Danny just wanted to get it over with, fearful of becoming a forty-year-old virgin like the nerd in the movie of the same name. He had flirted with some of his coworkers, but nothing had developed from it, even though two of the women seemed to have taken interest.

"That's a low blow, Dan," Tyler said, shaking his head. "I don't see her as some piece of meat for my first lay." He stood up and put his hands on his waist. "I guess I don't know what I see her as, in all honesty."

"Well, personally, I think it's kind of weird to date your dead roommate's ex, but whatever floats your boat I guess."

"Well, he's not really her ex—he died, it's not like they got in a fight and broke up. *That* would be wrong on my part. This is . . . different. I've been thinking about telling her about Amelia. Could be helpful to have a woman's perspective on all of this."

Danny jumped off his bed, eyes narrowed as they focused intensely on Tyler. "Under no circumstance should you ever do that. This is our thing, Ty. You really want to contribute another person to believe in Amelia? Then she'll tell all of her stupid friends and it will spread like wildfire. Those girls are so high school. Within a month the entire campus will know about Amelia Doss."

"Whoa, man, simmer down. I didn't say I was going to tell her for sure, just considering it. Besides, it's not like you own the rights to Amelia Doss. I can tell whoever I want if I think it will help our cause. It's not like the police are looking into a century-old axe murderer."

"You're playing with fire, Ty."

"*I'm* playing with fire? You're the one who let this bitch out of the grave in the first place. You should be glad you have someone who wants to help you figure this out, or else you could go at this alone."

Danny balled his hand into a fist, his arm trembling with rage as he fought to control his emotions. He understood neither of them were thinking rationally in the heat of this moment. Both were sleep-deprived, worried, and stressed beyond comprehension. But none of that excused Tyler from wanting to make a regrettable decision. Not only did Danny have zero trust toward Ella, it wasn't anyone else's business what they were looking into.

The two stood face-to-face, Danny easing his fist as he relaxed his rushing thoughts. "I'm sorry I snapped. I'm under a lot of pressure."

"I get it, don't worry. And I'm going through some things, too. My roommate is gone. Forever. It's put some things into perspective. I don't want to wait around for life to come to me. Sometimes you need to go out and make life happen for yourself. So what if Ella is way out of my league? I just might pursue her and see where it takes me. Worst thing that can happen is she's not interested and nothing changes. It's literally a low-risk, high-reward scenario."

Danny shrugged. "If you say so, man. I just think you need to tread carefully—there's still something off about her, if you ask me."

Tyler shook his head and crossed the room toward the door, turning around to face Danny. "I thought you were my friend. All I expect from you is a little support on this sort of thing. I get it, you found the body, and it was my roommate. We're both coping. But we are still friends and need to be there to support each other through life—I'm not getting that feeling from you right now. Just seems to me you're jealous that I might have a shot at getting with a girl like Ella."

Danny scoffed. "Excuse me? No, Ty, *you're* way out of line. I'm not jealous of that slut. You can date whoever you want. I was just giving you my opinion—as your *friend*—about her. I don't like her. Not one bit. There, I said it as plainly as I could. You still have the right to date her—I can't stop you, but you'll never have my support. I think she's wrong for you. I think she's hiding something. I don't trust her—she's too fake. I just wish you would see through that, but she has you wrapped around her skinny little fingers already."

"No, she doesn't even know I'm interested—that's impossible."

"But she does, Ty. Look at what she's done already. Listen to us, fighting over nothing. She's already causing problems in this friendship that has been going over ten years strong. Don't let her live in your head rent-free. Don't lose sight of who you are."

"I'll always listen to your opinion, Dan, but that doesn't mean I have to agree. Sometimes you take shit too far. You don't even know her and are sticking to the assumptions you've already made. And I know you'll never allow yourself to change your mind because you can't bear the thought of being wrong about anything!"

"Get the hell out of my dorm!" Danny snarled, pointing to his door. "Call me when you're ready to act like an adult."

Tyler shook his head and stormed out of the room, slamming the door hard enough to make dust puff out from the edges.

"Dammit!" Danny shouted through clenched teeth, kicking his trash can across the room. He returned to his bed and threw himself down, needing a moment to collect his emotions.

He had come so far in his research on Amelia, stemming back to his days in Ridgeway. Why Tyler wanted to risk throwing it all away was beyond his comprehension. He supposed, in time, his friend would come back to his senses and realize what a mistake it would be to loop anyone else in at this point, especially a slimy, untrustworthy person like Ella.

"It's just me for now," Danny said to himself. He sat up, his head heavy with stress. In his backpack waited the screenplay he had so eagerly wanted to work on upon arriving home, but now he had no desire, feeling an itch to hurry and understand how Amelia had tailed them to Denver, and where she might be lurking.

Danny dragged himself to his desk and fired up his laptop, leaning back in his chair and gazing out the window as he did so. The days were shorter, and the sun had already started to go down, splashing an orange glow across the sky. Somewhere outside that window was Amelia Doss, hiding in an alley, waiting to slash a homeless person's throat for the sheer joy of it.

The thought made Danny nauseous, the glow from his

laptop screen making his head spin. He had to power through to continue his research, which he had left off on studying a map from Ridgeway to Denver, trying to make sense of how Amelia could have arrived in town. Knowing that even in her bodily resurrection, she would still have been true to her original self. Automobiles would have still been considered a luxury when Amelia had died, so she may have had access, but it wasn't likely.

"Another dead end," Danny whispered, growing frustrated that the more he looked into different aspects, the less he seemed able to eliminate as possibilities.

He stared at the map, the vast mountain range looking back. Amelia could have walked the entire way, hiking through the hills of the Rockies, avoiding the roads altogether. It would have taken her an eternity, but she had already proven to have the survival skills to last in such a scenario, especially if she moved during the summer.

Danny stood up, needing to pace around the room to think more clearly. "That doesn't make sense. It would be three days of continuous walking. That's ludicrous."

But he soon understood it wasn't as crazy as it seemed. Amelia wasn't a human being. She didn't require food, water, or rest, as far as he knew. She *could* walk for three days straight if it meant getting revenge on him and Tyler. He shook his head.

"She has to have help."

He moved to the window, looking outside but not *seeing*. If Amelia grew stronger as more people believed in her, it was almost certain she could return to her original appearance. Her wounds would heal, her deathly stench vanish, leaving a regular 20-year-old woman. Once in that state, she could have easily traveled to another mountain town where no one would recognize her and get herself cleaned up. Hell, she could have done the same thing in Ridgeway.

People only knew the legend, not what she actually looked like.

Danny dashed back to his computer, sifting through his saved files of research. He had a folder dedicated to the old images he had scanned at the Ridgeway library. He hadn't forgotten what Amelia looked like, but wanted a clear picture to see.

He found the one he wanted and enlarged it across the screen. Amelia stood alone, her long black hair dangling to her chest. In the image, she had a soft smile, pale skin, and bags under her eyes. It had been taken shortly after her capture, days before the town hung her.

"What would you look like today?" Danny asked the screen. He closed his eyes and tried to imagine her with a shorter haircut, dressed in modern clothing instead of the flowing, flowery housedresses she seemed to don in all the pictures.

"Son of a bitch." Danny's eyes shot open and he minimized the photo, promptly opening Facebook and typing in Ella's name in the search bar. He expanded her profile picture and had to click through a couple until finding one that showed her entire face—the first few showed her with a drink to her lips in each. When he landed on one, he pulled open the picture of Amelia next to it, studying the two side by side.

Danny leaned forward and brought a fist to his chin. They had similar traits, but the closer he looked, he still couldn't draw any concrete conclusions. While Amelia appeared to have jet-black hair, Ella's was dark brown with red highlights. They both had pale skin, and the eyes appeared somewhat similar, but the original picture of Amelia was too old and grainy to provide true clarity.

You're just thinking crazy now.

"I'm not. Amelia is closer than we all think."

He closed Ella's picture and scrolled down her feed, not taking too long to find that her profile hadn't been created until August, just a couple of months ago. Danny furrowed his brow as he read it again to make sure he wasn't mistaken, wondering why a college freshman would have barely opened an account.

She only had twenty-three friends listed, and random pictures of her at parties. If he didn't know any better, he would have thought it was a fake account. He supposed her parents could have kept her sheltered, and she didn't get to create an account until getting to college, but she didn't seem the type. And for as popular as she had become in just a couple of months, why less than two dozen friends?

"Who are you really?" Danny asked, about to fall down a rabbit hole of research that would prove challenging to emerge from, like a bottomless grave.

❧ 16 ❧

lla had the key to Tyler's dorm room and could have killed him at any time while he slept. She could have done it silently with no one hearing a thing. It was simply a matter of severing the windpipe and cutting the jugular. He would bleed out in peace, and by the time they found him, she would have been long gone with no one the wiser. However, Ella enjoyed the hunt; she relished in the games. She often imagined the surprised look on Tyler's face; a realization of horror so great that when she killed him, that mask of horror would remain forever frozen there in death. Yes, the only thing that would make Tyler's death a satisfying one, would be if she took her time, let him get close to her, and then struck when least expected it.

Now, she made her way up the stairs, guys calling out greetings to the girl they knew as the life of the party. Ella smiled and waved, and said hi as she passed them, and soon stood at Tyler's door. She knocked. A wave of déjà vu flooded over her. She'd found herself at this door with increasing frequency.

There was a shuffle from somewhere within, and Tyler opened the door. Just as he'd said, Jason's side of the room had been stripped bare; his belongings likely sent back to his family. At least now, Ella had Tyler to herself.

"Hi!" she said, her tone upbeat, friendly. She'd worked for hours in front of a mirror to get the cadence exactly right.

"Hey, Ella." Tyler smiled and opened the door wider so she could come in. His desk lamp was on.

"Ugh, studying?" She glanced at the open book on the table.

"Yeah." He motioned to the chair at the now empty desk across the room.

But Ella just looked at him.

"Oh." He hurried to the desk, pulled out the chair, and brought it to the center of the room for her to sit. "I don't know why I thought it would be good to talk to you from across the room."

She let out a laugh, pulled off her backpack, and sat. "It's okay. So how are things?" She'd only seen him the day before, but it seemed a good segue into a conversation.

"The same really." He narrowed his eyes at her and as if speaking a thought aloud asked, "How is it a small-town girl is so popular?"

With a shrug, she set her backpack on the floor next to her. "To be honest, I never was popular growing up. So, it's kind of fun." She wasn't lying. Being one of the most popular girls on campus, next to those perky, wretched cheerleaders, was fun. She never wanted it to end, even though she knew that once she'd killed Tyler, she'd have no choice but to move on. "I'll enjoy it while it lasts."

He gave her a quizzical look. "While it lasts?"

"Well, it's doubtful my popularity as the life of the party will extend beyond college. Right? At some point I'll just be another girl working a nine-to-five job." Letting out a wistful sigh, she tipped her head to one side. "Why do you always look so haunted?"

Tyler flinched back for a moment and blinked, as if the question had startled him. "Just a lot on my mind, I guess."

"No, it's not that. You have mannerisms of someone who's dealt with a lot of tragedy."

"Oh?"

"I've seen it before. There was a farmer who lived in our town who lost his wife to cancer and his daughter to a car accident in the span of a few months, and he had that look," she said, proud of herself for having come up with such an insidious lie out of thin air.

Tyler frowned. "Danny didn't think I should say this, but you know—maybe it's time I tell you." He sat down across from her and rubbed his hands together as if debating how to phrase whatever he was going to say. "I grew up in a town where an infamous serial killer went on a murder spree back in the early nineteen hundreds."

She widened her eyes on cue. "Yikes. I bet that makes for a lot of local legends, huh?"

He ignored her comments and continued. "Last year, my friend, Bryson Day, was murdered. So were a few others. A local shopkeeper, a drunk guy in an ally, and one of my teachers. Then the killer kidnapped my mom, and Danny and I almost died trying to save her." He pursed his lips together and looked at her, waiting for a response.

"Wow." She swallowed carefully. "Copycat murders?"

"You're going to think I'm crazy..."

Ella bit her lower lip. "Well, I don't think that you're prone to crazy thoughts, so..."

He let out a heavy sigh. "We think Danny raised the murderer from the dead, and we think she's the one who killed Jason, and who has been killing homeless people throughout Denver."

She folded her hands in her lap. What would Ella say? But she couldn't think of anything.

"See? I knew you'd think it was crazy." He leaned back in the chair, a look of defeat in his eyes.

"A woman serial killer?" She bit her lower lip again, thinking back to a documentary she'd watched about female serial killers. "You realize how rare that is, right? But... wow. That's some heavy stuff."

"The indisputable fact is that Ridgeway had a serial killer. A female serial killer named Amelia Doss. She was caught and hung for her crimes, but she's back. I don't know how, but I think she thinks I'm my dead ancestor. He was the guy who helped catch her and put her to death." He gave her a weak shrug. "I saw her when we were saving my mom. It was definitely her."

"Or maybe a copycat," she repeated. Then she put up her hands. "Okay, so let's say it is this serial killer, Amelia whatever, and let's just say, for the sake of argument, she's obsessed with you and wants to kill you. So why would she kill *Jason?*"

"To torment me," he said. "To get revenge."

She gave him a half-hearted smile. "But people can't come back from the dead."

"Like I said, I don't know how it happened, but it did. Trust me." He took on a defensive posture. "I wouldn't believe me either if I hadn't experienced it myself. Amelia Doss is as real as you and I, and she's here. By telling you, I've probably put your life in danger." He let out a heavy sigh. "I shouldn't have told you. Not only have I put you in danger, but if Danny is right and people's belief in her gives her power, then you're just one more person whose belief can feed her."

Ella fought back the smirk that threatened to erupt onto

her lips. Instead, she gave him a sardonic smile. "Well, I don't believe in this Amelia Doss. While I don't deny there is clearly someone out there killing homeless people, and someone killed Jason, we don't know it's the same person who did all those things in your hometown. Besides, how could a woman," she paused and tried to look a little distraught, but not too distraught. "Do that to Jason?"

He nodded. "Good point, unless she has supernatural powers or something. I mean, we are talking about a living corpse."

She faked a quick shudder. "It's like an actual horror movie. I hate those things." Then she began tapping her hands on her knees. The truth was Ella had seen horror films. She'd stayed up late a few times to watch them, and she found them quite enjoyable, if not comical. "Maybe we should pray. That's what my family always does when they face an unknown evil or need to quench a fear."

Tyler gave her a wary look. "Pray? Does it work?"

"No. Not really. Why do you think I wanted to move away from home? Of course, my parents don't know I'm an atheist, but I don't think I've believed in God since I was eight." Ella shrugged again. This was only a half-truth. She had stopped believing in organized religion by the time she was eight, and she always found it amusing to watch other people fake their own holiness on Sundays, when every other day of the week they sinned most fervently. But she believed in a god, and she was sure he'd bestowed upon her avenging angel status. When she was alive, in her time, she'd always heard the voices and seen the shadows. Surely only God could have sent them with a righteous message. Not much had changed in this modern world. The deeply religious were still horrible sinners, even when they pretended piety. Though now, more people admitted they didn't believe. Others only nominally believed in a higher power but weren't observant. It was an interesting change from her time. That kind of honesty gave her hope for humanity's future, despite how vile they were in every other way.

"I'm not religious either," he told her.

She nodded in understanding. "Then we don't pray. We just try to stay safe and keep our wits about us. I mean, if there is a killer loose on campus, anyone we know could be next."

Tyler shifted uncomfortably and then rubbed his bare arms as if trying to warm himself.

Knowing he was afraid sent ripples of pleasure through her. "Let's do something soon. Maybe dinner?"

He gave her a brisk nod. "Yeah, okay." It was all very non-committal.

"Perfect," she said. Then she glanced at her watch. "I should get going. My aunt's lawn guy is coming today, and I don't want to miss him."

They said their goodbyes and she left, her jaw set and the bloodlust roiling beneath the surface. There was only one thing that would satiate her. As she crossed the campus, taking the long way to the parking lot on the west side of campus, she came across a groundskeeper clearing out the low branches of trees, and dead branches of bushes before winter arrived. She decided to sit and watch him. It was always good to prune in fall.

The man wore heavy boots and thick blue overalls. His head was turned away from her, so she couldn't make out his features. She couldn't even see what his hair looked like since it was covered with a blue ball cap. He bent down, picking up dead branches from where they were piled next to the sidewalk, and put them, handful by handful, into a large trash can. From the bench where she sat, Ella contemplated how she would kill him. Just like that, Marcus Bilbee, fifty-two, was about to become her next victim, and he didn't even know it yet.

She followed him across the campus, staying far enough away that she was a chameleon against the campus backdrop, until finally, he entered a smallish looking building that appeared to be a garden shed of some sort. It was remote in that it was off the main paths and not visible, either. Tucked away between the three-story Arts building and the towering spires of an old church, she imagined few people even knew the shed was there. Glancing around, she saw no one about. The light was fading from the sky. It would be dark soon. She set her backpack behind a tree along with her jacket, removed her knife from her pocket, then slipped into the shed after him.

He wasn't very spry, though his strong hands did reach up and try to grab her hands, and the knife. But Ella was stronger. Renewed with vigorous strength, fueled by Tyler's fear of Amelia Doss, Ella subdued her victim, and he was soon bleeding out, gasping and flopping like a fish out of water until there was no struggle left in him. She waited until he stopped moving to undress him and carve out a portion of his bicep. The flesh was warm and wet, but somewhat grizzled. Despite this, she ate what she could, dropping a good portion of it next to the body. She was still hungry, so she took the knife and carved out his eyeballs, the blade sliding easily into the sockets, the bone helping to guide her as she removed each one. After excising the chewier bits, she slipped one of the eyeballs onto her tongue, loving how smooth it was, and how it popped in her mouth when she bit down on it. It was almost like a bonbon. Then she ate the second one. Satisfied, she wiped the knife, and her hands, on a piece of burlap, folded the knife back up, and put it into her pocket. Then she checked herself over. Surprisingly, she only had a small amount of blood splatter on her dark shirt. Nothing her jacket couldn't hide.

As quickly as she'd slipped into the shed, she glided out, put on her jacket and grabbed her bag, then sauntered casually back out to the main sidewalk.

17

"What's been going on?" Tyler asked. "I heard about Bryson, but nothing else."

He had called his mother, not having checked in with her in a couple of weeks and desperately wanting to know how Ridgeway was doing in regards to Amelia Doss.

"It doesn't feel like much has changed. People talk about her the way they always have. No one actually believes she is alive, even after my interview with the newspaper."

They had interviewed her for a special report on the call Sheriff Abbott had to make to the Old Lady Myers property in the spring. Wendy Reynolds had told the story from her perspective, not sparing any details of her kidnapping and being tied up in the basement. She committed to her story that it was Amelia Doss, but the residents dismissed it as tainted perspective. Surely Wendy was too flustered to see or clearly think in the heat of the moment. No one blamed her for the testimony, many believing she needed to seek mental help to sort through the events of that night.

Regardless, the article had sparked the rumor mill in what eventually led to Amelia gaining further strength.

Wendy's skepticism had faded since the initial days of Tyler probing her about the legend. Now that she had witnessed the horror firsthand, she could no longer dismiss Tyler's inquiries.

"It just doesn't add up. If she's in Denver, then she must be at full strength, or very close. But that wouldn't be the case if it's been business as usual."

"I don't know, Ty. I can only speak regarding the circle of people I spend time with."

And that was true. She'd have no way of knowing if the legend had spread through the high school like a ravaging wildfire. Just because she lived in Ridgeway, didn't mean she knew about everything going on.

"I guess. How are you and Dad?"

"We're doing good. Finally getting into a new routine with just the two of us. We joined a bowling league on Wednesday nights, and go on dinner dates every Friday and Saturday. We miss you, but we're adjusting."

Tyler's father had called him after his first week at college, telling him to call Wendy often in the early days, as she spent most evenings crying into a bowl of Rocky Road ice cream. Tyler had done so and eventually learned when to ease off based on the gradual increase of joy he heard in his mother's voice. Today, she sounded like her normal self.

"How have things been since Jason? How is Danny?"

Tyler bit his lip at the mention of Danny. They still hadn't spoken in a couple days.

"Things are okay. Sometimes it's weird looking up and remembering I'm alone in this dorm, but I spend so much time doing schoolwork, it hasn't been too often. Me and Danny are sort of fighting right now."

"What happened?"

"A few things. It all started after he found Jason. I think we're both just stressed over that whole thing. Just in a funk, I guess, not seeing eye to eye on pretty much everything that comes up in discussion."

He refrained from telling his mother about Ella, still not sure what that relationship even was, also dodging the can of worms of a whole new conversation that could go on for hours.

"Well, I'm sorry to hear that, I hope you two get it all figured out. I'm sure you will."

"I'm not too worried. We just need some space, I guess."

"Let me know how it goes. I need to go get dinner ready. Are you still eating well?"

"Yeah, you know I don't skip meals no matter what's going on. Probably order a pizza tonight."

Wendy chuckled. "Live it up while you can, college boy. Talk to you again soon. I love you."

"Love you."

They hung up and Tyler remained on his bed, lying on his back just as he had during the phone call. He knew it was time to reach back out to Danny, but part of him thought it might be best for Danny to contact him first. After all, he was the one who had kicked Tyler out of his dorm room.

The fact they had been out of touch for so long had taken its toll on Tyler. He had woken up in the middle of the night on two different occasions, unable to pinpoint a reason. Even though he ate at all the usual times, his stomach always felt full, not craving anything since the moment he had left Danny's dorm.

The more he thought about it, the more frustrated he became. He understood why Danny didn't want to share any details with Ella, but couldn't get around the fact that he refused to consider Tyler's reasoning. If he could convince Danny that Ella could be trusted with the secret, she could prove plenty helpful in their quest to find Amelia. They could use her popularity as a weapon. She had connections all around campus in the way of friends and faculty, never mind the natural charm she could easily turn on like a light switch. While it appeared slimy on the surface, another reason Tyler was sure of why Danny hated her so much, Ella knew how to get what she wanted out of people. Now that Ella knew, he would have to tell Danny. Or find some way to convince Danny without telling him that he'd already told her. Then he'd have to convince Ella to help them. Which would be a challenge, since she didn't appear to believe a word he said.

If Amelia Doss was lurking around campus, either under-cover or simply by hiding until the night, Ella just might have the resources to extract information about the matter that wasn't being shared publicly with the student body, or even Danny's security team. Tyler hadn't even intended on telling Ella anything until consulting with Danny, but his stubborn refusal now served as a roadblock. Which is why he'd told her anyway.

"Danny has his research to do, but so do I," Tyler said to his ceiling. "We have different approaches—that's why it all worked and came together last time."

He knew his friend had developed a certain selfishness that blurred on the line of sole responsibility, since Danny had been the one to let Amelia out, but that didn't give him the right to force his methods through as gospel.

They'd have to get on the same page eventually, especially if they wanted any chance of bringing down Amelia for a second time. For now, he'd have to continue as he saw best, but Tyler also had the mental distraction of Ella.

She had developed such a pull over him since Jason's death, mainly the night she came to the dorm to be consoled. The thought of her made his heart race in a way that was foreign to him. He'd had minor crushes throughout high school, and he supposed he was undergoing a similar phase right now. But he already sensed it had the potential to grow into something much stronger.

Maybe he was ahead of himself, but Tyler could close his eyes and envision a future with Ella. Walking hand in hand across campus, meeting her for lunch between classes, exploring each other's tongues on one of the courtyard benches, just like every other happy couple had the joy of doing. He couldn't deny his feelings, respecting the fact he had felt nothing like them before. He'd never given a girl the time of day at any point in high school, never imagined what a relationship with one would be like.

Until now.

Ella changed everything with her mysteriousness, charm, and overall sex appeal. The fact she showed an interest in him fueled his self-confidence to uncharted territory. If he could win over a girl like Ella, what couldn't he accomplish in life? The thought brought a smile to his face, and Tyler jumped out of bed, rejuvenated with confidence, ready to move forward with his research, knowing he and Danny would smooth things over soon enough.

He needed to get out of the dorm, so packed his binder into his backpack and left for the library across campus. It was a warmer fall day with a slight breeze, so he threw on his Denver State hoodie before venturing out.

Campus always quieted after five o'clock, the bulk of classes done for the day. Traffic was light, but when he saw Ella strolling by the dorm building by herself, Tyler couldn't help but call out for her attention, his heart immediately racing as he approached her.

"Hey, Ella. How are things?"

Her face lit up, making Tyler's palms sweat as he rubbed them dry inside his hoodie's front pouch. "I'm done for the day and am heading home. Wasn't a bad day."

"Good to hear."

He paused and looked down to his feet, not sure what to say, paralyzed by his nerves that had taken hold of his simple functions. Ella giggled at the awkward silence.

"Where are you headed?" she asked, eyes scanning the backpack slung over his shoulder.

"Just to the library. Sometimes I need a change of scenery." He debated telling Ella about his fight with Danny, but decided it would lead to more questions he wasn't ready to address, at least not out in the open.

"Well, you have fun with that—I'm not looking at another book until tomorrow. I'll see you around."

She grinned before turning away, leaving Tyler disappointed in their encounter. He'd have to eventually step up and take charge of a conversation, possibly ask her out on a proper date. He'd had the perfect opportunity to, several times. And yet he'd chickened out. He vowed he'd do it the next time he saw her. Not just coffee or dinner in the dining hall either, but he still didn't know if the timing was right.

Tyler stood there a moment, watching Ella disappear into the parking garage, wondering if he could have changed anything. Doubt also crept into his mind. If she really had an interest in him, why would she cut off a conversation so abruptly? Wouldn't she have wanted to stay and talk, even through all of his awkwardness?

If I invited her to have dinner off-campus, would she have come?

The thought played over in his mind as he continued to the library, no longer interested in diving into his research, his mind too consumed with how to best approach Ella the next time they crossed paths. He had her phone number, and could call her right now to apologize for acting strange.

He pulled out his cell phone and typed in Ella's name. They had never spoken on the phone, or even sent text messages to each other. He only had her number after she gave it to him during one of the parties they had gone to with Jason. He wasn't even sure if he had given his number to her.

"Dammit," he muttered under his breath, shaking his head. "Nope, you blew it. Back to the drawing board."

Tyler stomped away from his dorm, committed to spending at least thirty minutes in the library. Amelia always had a way of letting his mind freefall into research, and that was what he needed right now to distract him from all the other noise in his life. He'd spend the time figuring out the best way to tell Ella about all of his work on this subject, and also what would be beneficial for her to know.

He thought back to a lesson one of his high school teachers had taught during a sex education class. *Not everyone you connect with has the potential to be a romantic relationship. Some people will be friends, while others may be business partners, or mentors. There are so many roles we need fulfilled in our lives, and it's a travesty how many relationships go to waste because of the pursuit of romance.*

Tyler mentally repeated this mantra until reaching the library, supposing Ella might have a different role in his life than he originally thought.

18

Something about Ella kept nagging at Danny, which is why he agreed to sweep the admin building when O'Brien had asked for volunteers. The buildings were never dark as there was security lighting, although dim, in every office. So, it was easy to slip into the main administration office and find a computer that was still on, and better yet, one with a password on a sticky note hanging on the cubicle wall. He looked up Ella Jones. It was all there, or at least what Tyler had told him. She was from Archer, Wyoming. Her birth date, a suspicious January first, put her at twenty-one years old. Her high school, Archer High. Then Danny did something he never thought he'd do. He printed her entire record. Transcripts, schedule, enrollment application, and the record of special dispensation she'd gotten to live off-campus as a freshman. She apparently lived with an aunt. Betty Mathers. It also had her address. When it finished printing, he exited the student database, took the papers from the printer, and slid them inside his jacket, then went about going through the building. He finished five minutes before his shift was over and already knew what he'd tell Tyler if he asked how Danny had gotten the information. A friend had helped him get it.

He clocked out and hurried back to his dorm room, his mind racing with a million questions. Why hadn't she started school when she was eighteen, or even nineteen if she'd gotten a late start? Why twenty-one? Avoiding eye contact with anyone, he practically sprinted into his dorm and locked the door behind him. He pulled the printout from his inner jacket, still in mild disbelief that it had been that easy, and looked over the pages again. Ella was an 'A' student. She wasn't Amelia Doss. But who *was* she? He didn't like that Tyler was so enamored with this girl. A few minor details about her life, and Tyler was besotted. It was shameful, really.

He knew then that he owed it to Tyler, despite their disagreement, to at least find out all he could about Ella. Because if she was lying to Tyler, he had to know. Danny didn't want to see his best friend get hurt, even if he was being a stubborn asshat.

When he sat down at the computer and typed in Archer, Wyoming, his heart sank when he discovered it was an actual place. Was it possible he was being paranoid? Perhaps even jealous that Tyler was interested in someone extremely attractive? He let out a heavy sigh. He found the Archer High School website and poked around. There was nothing but current student photos and activities there, and he didn't have the ability to hack it. What would he find anyway?

Then, in a futile attempt, he typed in *Ella Jones, Archer Wyoming*. Nothing. He glanced up at his browser's favorites bar, the social media icon beckoning him. He clicked it, logged into his account, then typed her name in the search bar. Ella popped up, her profile picture a party shot of her and two other hotties holding bottles of Coors and smiling into the camera, their cleavage leaving little to the imagination. Next, he scrolled through her pictures, one after another. Photos of her and every popular girl on campus, it seemed, filled the page. There were pictures of her with guys, of course. The football team. The hockey team. The baseball team. Danny groaned. Good God. She really knew everyone.

He'd looked at her social media before but decided to look again. Nothing seemed out of the ordinary. It was all the usual shit college students posted about. "What if we go back three years?" He clicked the search option, hoping to find a list of years to browse through, but there was still nothing. The account had been made in August just like it said the first time he'd visited the page, nothing had changed. "Why would it have been?" he asked to himself. Danny still found it all incredibly weird. Who in this day and age waited until they were twenty-one to start a social media account? He checked other social media sites, but if Ella had any of those, he didn't find any. Even looking for alternative accounts was no use. Those that could have been incognito or old accounts weren't searchable, which meant her social media was a dead end. Her parents' names were nowhere in her records. But the aunt...

He typed in *Betty Mathers, Denver Colorado*. Nothing. Then he typed the aunt's name and the exact address. All that came up was a vague property ownership record from the county public records website, but nothing else. How was it none of these people, especially Ella Jones, had no web footprint? "Weird," he whispered to himself. It was almost as if Ella Jones was a wraith with no past who'd slipped into their lives, and Danny didn't like it. He was going to have to think on it.

Meanwhile, he caught a faint odor on the air, and upon investigation, realized it was himself. He'd been so stressed about stealing Ella's records, he'd been sweating. He slipped Ella's records into his desk drawer, closed his laptop, and went to take a shower. Perhaps he'd get some ideas there. Shower ideas were some of his best. Instead, he found his mind wandering to his screenplay, and which actors could reasonably play the parts of him and Tyler. By the time he finished, he found himself more interested in working on his script than investigating Ella. Some popular girl could wait; inspiration could not.

⚜

THAT NIGHT HE HAD A DISTURBING DREAM. IN IT, ELLA and Amelia Doss were best friends. Amelia with her pale face and dirt-encrusted hair and fingernails stood next to Ella brandishing an axe, and yet Ella behaved like this was particularly normal. She was her usual cheery self. "Have you met my friend, Amelia?" she asked.

Dream Danny stood frozen in terror and disbelief. Why couldn't Ella see she was friends with someone who was literally an axe murderer? He tried to scream and couldn't.

"Let's go to a party!" Ella said.

"Yes. Let's play," Amelia said, her voice sounding like the demon possessing Regan in *The Exorcist*.

Danny shot straight up in bed, a sheen of cold sweat covering his body. He gasped for air, hands to his chest as if that would help to slow the violent pounding of his heart. "Shit," he said into the darkness. It was a ridiculous idea— that Ella and Amelia were in cahoots. What could a serial killer and a party-girl have in common? The question after that was, could Amelia control another person's mind? Evidence didn't appear to support that theory, but Danny held onto it. He fell back into his pillow, his heart rate slowing, and drew in a deep breath. When he realized it was only another hour before his alarm went off, he got up anyway and got ready for his day. Breakfast in the cafeteria didn't sound too bad, but first he had to make a phone call.

Getting Archer High School's phone number from the Internet took less than a minute, but it was eight in the morning and the school was open. Danny cleared his throat and lowered his voice an octave. "Hello, my name is Professor James at Denver University. I have been tasked to retrieve a few missing student transcripts from our records."

"Of course. What's the name?" the woman on the other end of the line asked.

"It's for Miss Ella Jones," he said, then gave the woman Ella's birthday. "She graduated three years ago according to the general record I have here."

"Let me check. Ellen Jones."

"No, Ella." He spelled it out to her.

"Oh. No, I don't have any student by that name."

"Is there a way to check in different years?" His frown deepened.

"Well, the database has all the students in it for the last thirty years. We have two Joneses. Michael and Robert. No female students at all." She paused. "Are you sure you have the right school?"

"I suppose it's possible. Don't worry, I'll get with the student and verify the information, then I'll be in touch if need be. Thank you for your time." He hung up. Ella Jones had become that much more suspicious.

He arrived at the cafeteria just after eight-thirty in the morning.

"They're not open today," some guy told him as he exited the door.

Danny furrowed his brow in confusion and went in anyway. A long line of yellow police tape blocked off the kitchen and food line of the cafeteria. He turned around and started back into the gray morning, wondering what happened.

"Danny!"

He heard his name and turned toward the woman's voice. It was Ella, sitting at one of the outside tables with a cup of coffee from the Tivoli coffee shop.

"If you're looking for breakfast, the food cart with burritos is up by the art building, and the Tivoli restaurant is open," she told him.

"Do you know what happened?"

Ella's expression turned grave. "I heard one of the cafeteria ladies is dead. It was Mrs. Casey."

"Jesus Christ." It came out of his mouth unbidden.

"They think she was murdered," Ella said in a hushed tone.

He swallowed at the lump forming in his throat. It was a morbid question, but he had to ask. "How did she die?"

Ella shrugged. "Dunno. They found her body in the freezer. Said it could have been there a week or longer, according to what I've overheard sitting here."

Danny's knees went a bit wobbly, and he made his way to the chair across from her. He wanted to look her in the eye. "Does it ever scare you? Being on campus with all these murders happening?"

"Definitely a far cry from my hometown," she said, opening up a perfect opportunity for Danny to ask more questions.

He didn't. Instead, he asked, "So how are you doing?"

She nodded. "Fine, but a bit tired."

"All that partying?"

"That and studying. How is Tyler?" The look in her eyes revealed concern, and that caused Danny to relax a bit.

"We had an argument, so..." He stopped himself. It was no one else's business that he and Tyler had an argument, so he changed the subject. "What's up with you and Tyler anyway? Are you a couple or something?"

A hint of crimson flushed her cheeks. "Nothing like that. I mean, I'd like to date him, and we've had coffee and lunch together here on campus, but I was taught that girls don't ask guys out. My family is very traditional and religious like that."

Surprised and intrigued, Danny leaned on the table with his forearms. "Well, if you're going to wait for Tyler, you could be waiting awhile. He's kinda shy. He never told me your family was religious."

"It's not something I broadcast," she said. "No internet, no social media. I think my parents expected me to get married right out of high school. If they'd had their way, I would have been homeschooled. Took me a few years to save up enough just to start college, and luckily my aunt is letting me live with her, which makes it more affordable."

In one fell swoop, Ella became even more of a mystery. While it didn't explain her non-existent transcript, some of the other things he'd found made more sense. Why she didn't have a past Internet presence. It also explained the wild party-girl persona. If Ella had only been recently freed of an oppressive religious environment, it made sense she would let her hair down at the first sign of freedom. But it still didn't explain why she'd lied on her college application. It was all a little too perfect. Too rehearsed. "That sucks."

"At least I didn't have a close encounter with a murderer though," she added.

Danny drew back, and for a second, it felt as though his heart stopped. "H-how did you know about that?"

She cringed. "Sorry. Tyler told me. Don't worry, I haven't told a soul. I can't even imagine what you guys must have gone through. It sounds horrific."

Damn it! Tyler had told her anyway. Just when he thought he was about to soften up and maybe even apologize to Ty, the anger came racing back. He let out an exasperated sigh. "You realize you're now in danger, right?"

She shook her head. "He told me all of that and apologized profusely for it. But as I see it, since I don't think it was Emily whatever-her-name-is, then she can't gain power, right?"

"Amelia Doss," he corrected. "Whether you believe is irrelevant. She has a tendency to go after people close to Tyler." Then he frowned. "And why do you say you don't believe? I was there. I can assure you it was her."

"Well, because the dead can't rise from the grave." Now she was just being snarky. She shook her head. "It seems more plausible that it was a copycat killer. While rare, I suppose a woman could be a copycat."

He pressed his lips together, not sure what to say. "Well, be careful, and if you're on campus after dark, call me or Ty and one of us will walk you to your car."

"Thanks," she said, throwing him a small smile. Then her expression changed. It was as if she'd had a horrible thought. Danny just didn't know how horrible until it came out of her mouth. "You don't think maybe the hamburger tasting funny had anything to do with that cafeteria worker, Mrs. Casey, do you?" Her face paled a little and her hand went to her mouth.

"You mean..."

"Like what if we ate human meat?"

His stomach did a somersault. Why would she say something like that? "God, I hope not. That's really..." He wasn't even sure how to end that sentence.

"Sorry. Sometimes my mind just plays out worst-case scenarios." She glanced at her phone on the table beside her. "Anyway, it's almost half-past eight. I should really get to the library. I have a paper I need to finish by Friday." She stood and began collecting her things. Then she gave Danny a broad smile. "See you around!"

That change in demeanor, from eating human meat, to bright and cheerful, sent his internal alarm bells off.

He got up and slung his backpack over his shoulder. There was something really not right with Ella Jones, and Danny intended to find out what it was.

19

The idea to murder the football coach came to her when she saw him patting a young female student on the rear. Men could be such impulsive creatures. Their lascivious intentions marked by the lust in their eyes. Coach Ellington looked like a drunkard. He was a heavy-set man with sunken eyes, red cheeks, and a flush of color on the tip of his nose. And by the looks of him, he was all hands. Ella frowned.

"Look at all those hotties on the field," Rachelle said from the bleacher space next to her. It was a chilly night and Rachelle wore a thick mahogany-colored jacket, a black pair of knit gloves, and a too-big cream-colored scarf.

Ella merely glanced over at her before her eyes settled on the coach again. He did it a second time. Casually dipped his hand down and cupped the buttocks of the young, blond-haired woman standing next to him with the clipboard. This time, the woman sidled away and threw him a glare that he didn't seem to acknowledge. It was, in part, men like Coach Ellington that had inspired her to go on a murderous rampage to begin with all those years ago.

"What are you scowling at?" Rachelle's voice pulled her back to reality.

She snapped out of it. "Oh, nothing. Thinking about an assignment."

Rachelle looked her up and down. "I can't believe you're not cold."

Ella laughed. "High metabolism, I guess. I'm rarely cold," she said. *Of course, being brought back from the grave shields one from the cold*, she thought. There were a lot of annoying and disgusting human things she no longer had to contend with. Menstruation. Urination and defecation. Cooking. Temperature changes. Though she was more than capable of pretending all of them if she wanted to. She'd even somehow feigned embarrassment in front of Danny, and he'd bought it. *I could have been in the theater*, she thought with a satisfied smile. When she thought of Danny, her mind turned to Tyler.

Rachelle poked her arm. "See? Number forty-two? That's Lance."

"What a horrible name," Ella mumbled.

A cackle tumbled from Rachelle's throat. "Girl! You're so *bad*."

Ella just gave her a knowing smile because she wasn't quite sure what the joke was. "Speaking of guys, do you think I should ask Tyler out or wait for him to ask me out?"

"You haven't asked him out yet?"

"Call me old-fashioned."

"I thought you asked him to dinner or something."

Ella shrugged. "If you call eating in the dining hall with friends a date. I was thinking something away from campus. With waiters."

Her friend snorted. "If you're waiting for him to ask, you could be waiting awhile."

She turned to Rachelle. "Why do you say that?"

"He seems like the shy, insecure type." Rubbing her gloved

hands together, a look of excitement washed over Rachelle's face. The game was starting.

Elle couldn't have cared less about football. She was only there because it seemed to be an important event among all her newfound party friends. "Maybe," she said. Then she drifted off into one of her many fantasies of hanging Tyler up and disemboweling him, while all around her, the crowd hooted and hollered and cheered. Ella blocked all of it out. Eventually the game would end, until then, she sat quietly with her thoughts, a small smile resting on her lips.

It was hours later when Rachelle grabbed her arm. "Great game! Though you were soooo busy thinking about Tyler. How much did you actually see?"

If Rachelle only knew. "Football is not really my game. I just came to hang out."

"We should totally go to Tony's. Best afterparties anywhere!" Rachelle stood up and grabbed her bag. Around them, the crowd began milling and filing from the bleachers.

"It's a Thursday night," Ella protested. She had plans, and Rachelle was stepping all over them.

"And?"

"And I promised my parents a phone call tonight," she said, not realizing how lame the excuse sounded until it came out.

"So, call them on your cell phone from outside."

"Good point. How about I catch up with you in about two hours?"

Rachelle gave her a surprised look. "Okay." Then a sly smile slid on her lips and she tossed her long dark locks over her shoulder. "This wouldn't have anything to do with Tyler, would it?"

Ella didn't confirm or deny the allegations. "Two hours." That should be all the time she needed to deal with Coach Ellington.

"All right, but if you're not there by ten, I'm blowing up your phone," Rachelle warned. "Later." Then Rachelle ran off, waving at someone she saw at the bottom of the bleachers.

Ella looked at her phone. Notification after notification popped up with party details, new social media posts, and text messages asking her where she would be. She slipped the phone into her pocket and finally left the bleachers as one of the few stragglers. She waited near the entrance until the only two people left on the field were her and Coach Ellington. Pulling a small notepad and pen from her purse, she started toward him just as he headed in her direction with his clipboard to his chest. To leave, presumably. "Coach Ellington! I'm with the campus newspaper, and I'd love a few quotes about how you feel the game went tonight."

"Yeah, all right." He gave her the once-over with eyes that were set too close together. "Why don't you come with me to my office."

There was a strange click, and the hum of the lights went quiet as the field lights and scoreboard turned off. Perfect. Now the shadows would come. It was as if the mere thought of them summoned them. She smiled.

He reached out and put his arm around her. "Don't worry, sweetie. I'll protect you."

But who's going to protect you? she thought. Then she patted her pocket. "Oh crap. I think I dropped my phone."

Coach Ellington withdrew. "Well, let's go back and get it. Damn things cost an arm and a leg."

She led him back onto the now mostly dark field, and he waited while she ran back up the bleachers where she'd been sitting and pretended to find her phone. Slipping it out of her pocket, she held it up. "Found it!"

"We're here, Amelia," the shadows chorused. She could see them drifting from beneath the bleachers and across the field, closing in a wide circle around the coach who hadn't yet noticed that something wasn't quite right.

"Thank you so much for coming back with me. My parents would kill me if I lost this thing," she said, giving him another gracious smile.

He held out his hand to help her down the last step. "It's not a problem. A pretty girl like you shouldn't be out here, alone in the dark." Then he put his arm around her waist. "Let's get you a few quotes for the newspaper."

His touch repulsed her, and she fought the urge to kill him right there. No, timing was everything. She had to distract him a little. "Did you always want to become a football coach?"

The coach chuckled. "I was in the big leagues. Damn knee injury first season after I signed with the Seahawks. But that was years ago. Decided to coach college ball instead," he said.

Ella doubted any of that was true. She may have been born in the first half of the twentieth century, but she knew when a man was lying in order to seduce a girl. But she would play his game. "That's so exciting. Did you have to have surgery? Do you have a scar?"

He smiled, pleased at her enthusiasm and naivety. "I'll show it to you if you like." Then he stopped abruptly. They were halfway between two sets of bleachers and he'd just realized that everything was completely black. When the shadows clamored in, all huddled together like they were, circling them like vultures, the thick darkness pulsated. And Coach Ellington was the carrion. He let go of her waist and turned around to where the safety lighting on the outskirts of the field should have been, but the shadows blocked it out completely. "What the hell?"

Ella, who could see just fine in the gloom, took out her knife, punching it right into the left side of his back, through muscle and bone. He fell forward with a cry. She turned to the shadow directly on her left. "It's a pity we don't have a spear to impale him on."

The shadow cackled, the ones around it joining in until they all laughed together and Coach Ellington, still screaming on the ground, put his hands to his ears to stop the infernal noise.

She towered above the fallen man, lifted his head, and drew the blade over the jugular, careful to stay out of the way. Some blood splatter couldn't be helped, but she'd learned where to stand and how to cut in order to dodge the spray. Standing back, she pulled a tissue from her purse and wiped the blood from her knife and slipped it back into her pocket. The bloodied tissue found its way into the outer pocket of her purse. She waited until his body stopped twitching before looking at the audience of shadows, who sat quietly waiting for her to speak.

"We need a few things," she said. Then she listed them, and the shadows got to work. The first thing they did was turn off the lampposts lining the outskirts of the field. Another shadow brought her some rope. From where, Ella didn't know and wasn't sure she cared. She let the shadows do the heavy work, heaving the body toward the flagpole. For the task of undressing the man, she did the honors. She pulled out her knife again to make quick work of it, leaving the coach's blood-soaked garments in a heap beneath the flagpole. Then, using the rope, she and the shadows hoisted the corpse of Coach Ellington up, until his penis and testicles were easily within reach. Ella took the knife and first sliced off his manhood, then the family jewels. They parted from his body expeditiously thanks to Amelia's precise carving. She left the useless bits of flesh on the ground below, then motioned up with her right hand, and the shadows heaved the body further and further up the pole until the nude, castrated man hung at the top. Wiping off her knife with another tissue and slipping it into her pocket once more, she stood back a few yards and admired their handiworks. "Bravo, my friends. Bravo!" she applauded the shadows.

"Thank you, Amelia," one of the closer ones said.

Ella skipped across the field, her shadows dancing beside her, and drove home in the prideful bliss of a job well done. It wasn't until she'd undressed and changed into her pajamas that she bothered to look at her phone. So many messages. She answered Rachelle with a lame excuse that something else came up, to which Rachelle replied, 'Go get him, gurl!' She answered the rest with, 'sorry, can't make it.' No explanation. The only one who would hound her for an explanation was Rachelle, anyway. Everyone else, well, they were what her mother used to call *fair-weather friends*. People who were your friends in name only and didn't mind hanging out with you when things were bright. But they would all disappear when you fell on hard times. She started a load of laundry, then entered the dimly lit living room to find the shadows swaying and twirling, as if doing a macabre dance in celebration of death.

"Now, who wants tea?" she asked her shadow friends with cheer.

The shadows whispered inaudible replies, so Ella only poured one cup for herself. She sat down in her favorite chair and let out a contented sigh, watching the shadows continue to twirl and make merry. Lifting her teacup, she toasted them, then took a sip of the lovely brew. *It's really a shame my shadows don't like tea,* she thought. Then her mind drifted back to Tyler. "I'll definitely have to castrate Tyler, too, when the time comes," she said aloud, above the din of her constant companions.

✣ 20 ✣

Danny had never been to Ella's off-campus home, not having a reason or desire to. His research, however, had sparked enough suspicions that he wanted to look around the place, and possibly sneak inside.

As a member of the security team, he had entered the school's system in the dead of night and pulled Ella's class schedule, finding she was on campus from 10 A.M. through 2 P.M. every day, sometimes until five o'clock, depending on the day of the week.

Danny enjoyed playing detective, waiting outside where Ella was expected to arrive for class, and not leaving for her house until confirming she went inside the building. Once in the clear, he drove to her neighborhood a mere ten minutes west of campus, a community of old bungalow-style houses likely built in the forties or fifties.

A lot of older people lived in these types of neighborhoods, and this one didn't disappoint. He saw an elderly man hand watering his yard, and a slow-moving fragile woman knitting on her porch. Danny slowed as he pulled up, killing the engine, and drawing a deep breath while nerves worked into his gut and arms.

He knew she had an aunt, but based on a few things she'd said, it seemed the aunt was currently out of town. He assumed she didn't have any other roommates, considering Jason had spent time with her exclusively at her house instead of his own dorm. He also didn't know her neighbors. If they were older folks, like the ones he'd passed a block ago, they were likely nosy. With any luck, the neighbors would be out and he'd have privacy as he lurked around the property. Many factors were at play that could cause the police being called on Danny, but he had to push those negative thoughts away if he had any chance of learning valuable information on this trip.

Danny stepped out of the car, sliding a pair of sunglasses over his eyes, pulling his ball cap down to help conceal his face. He may have looked suspicious, but if he needed to flee in a hurry, no one would have a chance of getting a good look.

The sky had turned gray since he left campus, powerful gusts of wind blowing over the city all morning. Rain was expected in the evening, and Danny could smell it in the air as he drew one final deep breath before starting for the house. Some houses had carports, but Ella's didn't. Instead, six-foot fences sectioned the property, and trees and hedges separated front yards. If he could get to the path alongside the house, no one would see him. The other alternative was to act like he had a reason to be there.

He strolled down the path, taking confident steps like he belonged, and looked over his shoulder before knocking on the front door, just to make sure no one had tried following him. Adrenaline pumped in his fingertips, his vision pulsing in and out of focus as he braced for the unknown. If a room-mate or her aunt answered the door, Danny planned to ask if they needed cable service and get the hell out of there as quickly as possible.

He waited a minute, then knocked another time to be sure. No one came to answer, so Danny tried the doorknob in hopes of Ella having left it unlocked. He had no such luck and tried the window to his left, again rejected.

"God dammit," he muttered, glancing around to see if any neighbors were watching. His only hope was to go around back. At least then he'd have less of a chance for prying eyes to see what he was up to.

With a dramatic sigh, Danny left the front entrance and jogged around the house until reaching the well-kept back-yard. All the gardens were empty, the grass mowed. The rear of the house had a small patio attached with a table and two chairs. A grill stood off to the side, covered for the off-season. Danny crept close to the house, trying the windows one at a time before he came to the back door. His body trembling as he felt exposed, since either neighbor could easily have come onto their own back patios and caught him.

The sliding patio door was locked, but Danny's heart sunk into his stomach when he looked over to see the kitchen window cracked open three inches, his heart racing even faster as he realized if he wanted to enter the place, he had to crawl through that window.

About to look like a criminal, he thought, not acknowledging that the act itself was indeed a crime. His obligation was to understand Amelia Doss, and he had grown too convinced that there was some sort of connection between her and Ella. The Denver police still hadn't known about Amelia, leaving Danny and Tyler as the only two people in Denver who could provide insight on the matter.

Danny looked left to right three different times to ensure no neighbors had wandered out to their patios. The coast remained clear, and he checked behind him one last time for any lurkers glancing over the fences. He was truly alone, and slipped his trembling hand into the cracked window, sliding it open.

"Okay, you can do this," he whispered to himself, eyes seeming to dance in every direction before fully committing to breaking and entering. He slid over a folding chair and stepped on it to elevate his body level with the window. The opening was at least eighteen inches wide, plenty for him to fit, but still a tight squeeze that could leave him with his legs dangling out of the window for a moment.

What if someone looks over their fence at that exact moment? he wondered. *I'd go straight to jail.*

Sweat had formed around his crown and he brushed it away with his arm, still debating turning away and forgetting about this whole thing. There had to be a better way into the house. Hell, maybe he could ask Ella, and she'd let him in with Tyler.

Danny shook his head. "It has to be now."

He propelled himself upward and reached into the window, pulling himself through. He got the top half of his body through the window in the first motion, his hands flailing around for a grip on the kitchen sink that had fortunately been left empty. His arms bulged as he pushed against the inside wall, allowing the rest of his body to fly through the window in a seamless motion, planting his feet inside the sink, sitting inside of it like an oversized child waiting for a bath.

Danny hopped down, holding up his weight on the counter to ensure his landing created no sound. He spun around and closed the window, growing disoriented by the minute thanks to his panic and paranoia running out of control. He paused and held his breath, wanting to listen for any sounds within the house, footsteps or a TV from another room, perhaps.

Nothing but beautiful silence filled his ears, and he gradually felt more relaxed that he was indeed alone.

Okay, one room at a time. Look for any clues, then get the fuck out.

From the kitchen, Danny saw the living room and a hallway that seemed to split in two directions. The house was small, but presumably had a basement. The place was kept a little too clean for Danny's liking. Ella was a college student, but there wasn't so much as a dirty dish in the sink, a stray sock on the floor, or an empty pizza box next to the trash can.

The refrigerator only had a couple of magnets on it for local restaurants, and a single photograph of Ella and Jason. He opened the fridge, curious. A gallon of orange juice and milk stared back from the top shelf, a carton of eggs, and what appeared to be a roll of ground beef. Ella had the bare minimum necessities, but oddly no beer, considering how much she enjoyed drinking it at the parties they had gone to. "Maybe the aunt is religious, too?" he muttered.

Danny rummaged through the cupboards, scrunching his face as he found three of them completely empty except for four boxes of tea, only one of them opened. One cupboard housed all the plates and glasses, one drawer below for all silverware. He shook his head. Something was not adding up. It seemed like no one lived here regularly.

Convinced she was hiding something, Danny left the kitchen and started into the rest of the house. The living room had a lone couch along the wall and a recliner opposite it, both facing a small television mounted across the room. A coffee table stood in the middle of the room, nothing but a stack of *Cosmopolitan* and *Vogue* magazines on it.

A hallway broke off from the living room. He stepped into the hallway and heard a noise. It stopped him dead in his tracks because it sounded like people whispering. A shiver ran the length of his body. *It's your mind playing tricks on you,* he thought. There were four doors along the hallway. One of them, he assumed, led to the basement. Danny opted to check out the other rooms first, knowing Ella's bedroom would be his best bet for finding any clues.

His feet whispered over the carpet, and he avoided touching anything, even the walls, sure to not leave behind evidence that he had been inside. Danny stepped into the bathroom first, surprised to find it nearly as barren as the rest of the house. A hair brush and comb lay on the sink. He opened the mirror that concealed the medicine cabinet, finding one shelf full of makeup, the rest empty.

"What the hell?" Danny asked.

Ella had no toothbrush, toothpaste, nail clippers, or hand soap. None of the necessities he expected in anyone's bathroom. To his relief, he poked his head into the shower to find shampoo, conditioner, and body wash.

"Is she more basic than we've thought?" He thought back to the times they had gone out together and recalled Ella always dolled up with makeup and styled hair. She appeared to take good care of her hygiene, but browsing the bathroom planted doubt. "Maybe her religion doesn't allow it?"

Danny left for the bedroom, bracing himself for more confusion about the girl who had somehow grown in popularity across campus despite not washing her hands. In the first sign of a college student, he found the bed undone, sheets tangled and splayed in every direction. Aside from that, the room appeared immaculate. One dresser stood at the foot of the bed with nothing on its top shelf.

He wandered toward the closet and opened it to find all the clothes neatly hung, a rack of shoes along the bottom containing four pairs for different occasions. Danny squatted down, noticing mud-caked hiking shoes as the only true mess in the entire place. He picked one up and examined it, the mud clearly dried for a while.

Danny couldn't recall a time Ella had ever mentioned hiking, or any outdoor activity. She gave off a prissy vibe, one that made him believe she would run away from flies buzzing around her head. Not someone cut out for the outdoor life of camping and hiking.

"Could just be an old pair," he said, putting the shoe back and closing the closet door. The room smelled like the perfume Ella always wore, a faint vanilla scent that reminded Danny of walking into an ice cream shop.

He stood in the middle of the room, looking around as disappointment crept into his mind. The bedroom was supposed to be the jackpot for whatever he was looking for, and so far nothing had come up except for more questions surrounding the increasingly mysterious Ella Jones.

With his head hung low, Danny shuffled to the nightstand next to the bedroom's entrance and opened the top drawer. There were a pair of glasses, a pad of sticky notes, and pens scattered about. A yellow sticky note had been folded in half, writing across it that read: *Jason's dorm key.* Danny gasped when he saw this and picked it up, unfolding it to confirm the key was inside before stuffing it into his pocket for Tyler. He knew his friend had gotten into a fight with Jason over his decision to give Ella a key to their dorm and thought this would be just the thing to break their current impasse.

"This is turning into quite the waste of time," he muttered, slamming the drawer shut and heading to the second bedroom that smelled of lavender and contained the clothing and belongings of an older woman. The aunt. On the dresser was a photograph of the old woman and Ella looking a lot plainer than he'd ever seen her.

His nerves had finally settled by the time he reached what he assumed was the basement door, and started down the cold, dark stairwell. When he reached the bottom, a rotting stench rushed his nose, making him gag. His hand shot up to cover his mouth and nose.

"What the hell is *that*?!" he gasped, his stomach churning with disgust. The odor smelled like a mixture of rotting meat and a sewage leak. Danny grew dizzy as he looked around the basement, searching for the source. He found a light switch and flicked it on, illuminating the confined space.

The basement had the laundry units, a freezer, a futon, and a storage closet. He opened the closet to find stacks of boxes, but his eyes fell immediately to the axe leaning against the wall, dried blood caked around the blade.

"Holy shit!" He spun around and bolted up the stairs, disoriented from the smell, wondering how the hell it hadn't spread to the rest of the house. Danny had seen everything he needed. The stench left little doubt that a dead body was somewhere, but he couldn't stomach it any longer to keep poking around.

Refusing to crawl back through the kitchen window, Danny let himself out the front door, locking the bottom lock, and gasping for fresh, outdoor air as he closed the door behind him. He brushed his hands over his clothes, feeling like the stench had clung to every fiber of his shirt and pants. His body broke out with gooseflesh as he processed the reality of what he had just encountered. Ella had a dead body in her basement, yet he had no evidence to warrant a call to the police, especially since he had to break into her house to learn this.

Danny returned to his car, shaking his head in disappointment, but relieved to know he had found something useful. As he drove away, windows rolled all the way down despite the gusts of wind, he cracked a grin while beaming with pride that he had revealed one simple answer.

Ella is definitely connected to Amelia Doss.

21

Tyler returned to his dorm after another day of classes. He had new homework assigned, but nothing due tomorrow, so he splayed across his bed to let his mind and body unwind. During the day, he had sent Ella a text message to break the ice, starting off their sporadic conversation by asking how her day was going.

She had sent brief replies, but Tyler assumed she was too focused on her classes to engage. Once he returned to his dorm, she sent him a message asking what he had planned for the evening. Just reading the message made him flustered, resulting in him overthinking the best response to send. He wanted to balance seeming too available, but not completely closed off.

Going to spend some time in the library tonight. Have some things to finish up. Tyler debated asking her to join, but sent the message before adding more. Sitting in a silent library wasn't exactly first date material, no matter how appealing it sounded to an introvert like Tyler.

"Dammit," he said to his empty room. "Sounds too occupied."

He had hoped to navigate the conversation toward a potential dinner invitation, but decided he had fucked up that opportunity. The library trip wasn't a lie—he had planned on spending an hour or two there to continue his research on Amelia. After having gone twice, he came to appreciate the silence and focus the library provided, always a private corner in the massive space for him to fall into the research and not worry about wandering eyes.

Tyler tossed his phone on the bed and fired up his laptop just as a knock came from the door. He wasn't expecting anyone, and his heartrate immediately elevated as he thought it might be Ella. He still had no read on her feelings toward him—or anything, for that matter—so it seemed equally likely for her to randomly show up to his dorm as it would if he didn't hear from her for the next two weeks.

Tyler drew in a deep breath as he reached for the door and cracked it open. "Danny?"

His friend stood in the hallway, a baggy hoodie drooped close to his knees, backpack snug over both shoulders. His eyes had bags under them, his hair a spiky, frazzled mess.

"Can I come in?" he asked. "We really need to talk."

"Sure." Tyler stepped aside and pulled the door open all the way.

Danny shuffled in and promptly dropped his backpack on the floor. "I found something."

"Wait, are we not going to talk about what happened?" Tyler asked.

Danny frowned. "About our little spat? Ty, we had an argument. I've moved on, I hope you have, too. Nothing more to say."

Danny's bluntness caught Tyler off guard, leaving his mouth agape as he tried to think of a witty comeback. None came, and he sensed the urgency radiating from his friend.

"Okay. I'll just say that I'm sorry for how that unfolded and we can leave it at that."

Danny nodded. "Me too."

"So what have you found?"

Danny smirked as he rummaged into his hoodie pouch, pulling out a yellow sticky note and handing it over.

Tyler studied it, his brows furrowed, before grabbing it and seeing the words scribbled on the opposite side that read: *Jason's dorm key.*

"What? How?" Tyler asked, unfolding the note and seeing the spare key inside.

"I told you—we need to talk. You should probably sit down."

Tyler obliged and hurried to his desk chair, spinning around to face Danny. "Wait, so you met with her? You were at her house? I'm confused."

Danny chuckled. "After we got into that fight, I started digging into Ella. I figured Amelia Doss murdered Jason, so why not look into all connections? I didn't find any direct connections, but what I found still disturbed me. It appears all of Ella's history is fabricated. I have a friend on the security team who can pull any student's records. He helped me get Ella's, and down the rabbit hole I went. There is still more cross-checking I need to do—and I'm hoping you can help me—but so far it seems her entire high school transcript is fake. The school she claims to have gone to has no record of her. Her parents' names aren't in her records. Nothing was adding up, so I sneaked into her house to snoop around."

"You what?!" Tyler's eyes bulged as he stared across the room to Danny who remained standing, pacing as he spoke. "Dan, that's some serious shit. What if you got caught?"

Danny shrugged. "I didn't."

"Jesus Christ, so that's how you got the key."

"Yep, a bonus gift, I guess. At first, I couldn't find

anything. Her place is nearly empty—again, something that seemed off. I poked around, found nothing until I went into her basement . . . there is definitely a dead body in there, but I couldn't stick around to find it. The smell was . . ." He trailed off and shuddered, his face scrunched as if he had just sniffed a carton of rotting eggs.

"What does this all mean, though? How does it tie to Amelia?"

"That's what we need to figure out. I'm one hundred percent convinced now that there is a direct correlation between Amelia and Ella. There was a bloody axe in the basement closet. That's all I found before I had to leave. Once we find that link, we find Amelia."

"I should also tell you something else," Danny said, leaning forward. "I visited a few occult shops to research how to get rid of Amelia for good. The witches I talked to suggested that maybe Amelia is a demon."

Tyler paled. "Demon?"

"It's not that she was a demon when she was alive, but because she did so many horrific things while she was alive, she became a demon in death." Danny shook his head. "I'm wondering if Ella's weird religious upbringing didn't have something to do with Amelia, as a demon, attaching to her or something. If any of that is true, Amelia could control her. Possess her, even."

Tyler's stomach tightened, blood rushing from his chest. The thought of Ella having a connection to the serial killer, and Amelia possibly being a demon who wanted him dead made his flesh crawl with terror. That she knew where he lived just might keep him awake until they resolved this matter. He no longer felt safe in his dorm. "Where do we go from here?"

"I don't know, man, this is getting way too close. Again. We need to figure this out sooner than later."

"Library?" Even though he had already told Ella he would be in the library tonight, it still seemed a safer place than being confined to his dorm. If Amelia showed up at the library, they'd have multiple options for getting away. That wasn't the case if they stayed in his dorm.

Danny shrugged. "Fine by me. Let's go."

Tyler stuffed his laptop into his backpack and they headed out, sure to lock the door and double check it once they stepped into the hallway.

"Do you think Amelia is living with Ella?" Tyler asked in a hushed voice.

"It's possible, but I still didn't see anything that suggested someone else besides the aunt was living there. Could have been more to it in that basement, but we'll never know."

"Let's go back—we can plan to bring gas masks so we can breathe."

Danny shook his head vigorously. "I am never doing that again. I thought I was going to puke all over the porch. Guess I'm not cut out for life as a criminal. We just need to worry about finding the connection, then we can locate Amelia and finally take her out."

"I still think this could be to our advantage. I already told Ella about Amelia. None of the details. But I have to say, she seemed to react like any normal person would react. So she's not possessed." He paused and looked at Danny for any sign of anger.

"I already know you mentioned it to her because she mentioned it to me. You're right. She seemed completely clueless and so normal. She's probably not possessed, but there's a connection." Danny pursed his lips in deep thought as they stepped out of the building, the cool evening air carrying the smell of potential rain as gray clouds hovered in the distance. "That actually could work now that we have this new information. You can play dumb and talk about Amelia and keep watching how she reacts and see if she says anything."

"We can talk about it. Maybe we want to wait until we have a clear connection before putting her on the spot. The more information we have, the more ammo we'll have in any conversation with Ella."

"Honestly, Ty, once we have the connection, it's just a matter of luring Amelia and sending the bitch back to Hell. Nothing else to it. That's what I want to focus on tonight. We find that connection, we end this shit once and for all."

Danny picked up the pace and Tyler had to jog to keep up. They reached the library within two minutes and entered to find the place nearly deserted, maybe ten students scattered across the campus' third largest building.

The library had gone through an intense expansion and renovation two years earlier, now including thousands of additional books, new conference rooms, archives, and designated study areas strategically placed furthest from foot traffic.

They entered and Tyler took the lead, guiding them to an area in the far back corner where he had camped out during his prior visits. They settled at a table that seated four people, sitting diagonally to use the open chairs as foot rests.

Danny promptly pulled out his laptop and turned it on, his fingers tapping the table as he waited.

Tyler followed suit, leaning back in his seat and crossing his arms behind his head. "Do you think we need to be afraid of Ella?" he whispered.

"I'd probably avoid being alone with her, if possible, at least until we know what we're dealing with. She's an accomplice, as far as we know. Why take any chances?"

Tyler tried to imagine Ella sneaking out at night with Amelia, gallivanting through the streets of downtown Denver to hunt down the homeless population, slitting their throats and eating their limbs for sport. The thought seemed so absurd that it brought a smirk to Tyler's lips. "I don't know. I'm not about to invite her over for dinner in my dorm or anything like that, but I think she's harmless. She doesn't exactly have the smarts to be a serial killer and keep getting away with it."

"But she's working *with* a serial killer. A supernatural one with abilities we don't know about."

Tyler nodded, sitting forward and opening the word processing program on his computer. Their table stood along a window overlooking the science building, a short walkway separating the two. Tyler couldn't help but keep gazing out the window, certain Ella would show up at some point. His heart raced at the thought. *What would I even do if she walked up to this table?*

His emotions were still too mixed. She had a pull on him he hadn't quite figured out, even with the developing information of Danny's findings in her house. Part of him had every intent on one day pulling her in close, planting his lips on hers, discovering how she tasted. The other part of him wanted to turn and run as fast as possible.

He chuckled and shook his head free of the thoughts, needing to focus on the file now open in front of him.

"Do you want to see if you can find more about her aunt?" Danny asked. "I searched the internet for public information and found her name. But I'm curious to know if the house is paid for, or if Ella is on the deed. She doesn't have a job that we know about, right?"

Tyler shook his head. "Not that I've heard of. I'll see what I can find."

"Cool. I'm gonna keep searching her name and see if anything else comes up. Past jobs on LinkedIn, plus another look at her Facebook page. There's gotta be something I missed. Something we can work with."

"I can always ask her, try to position it as an innocent inquiry."

"Too risky," Danny said with an aggressive shake of the head. "We need to stay as under the radar as possible with Ella. Not saying to ignore her if she reaches out, but no need to be proactive right now. That's why I want to find out about her living arrangements. It would be easier if we could talk to her aunt. I'm going to see if I can find a copy of her initial application to the university—those require financial records. And if they're forged, then we're looking at a whole scandal that can really ruin her life."

Tyler recoiled at this, his eyes beaming into Danny.

"Don't worry," Danny said, raising a hand. "I'm not setting out to do that, just looking for that link to Amelia. To do that, we might have to dig deeper than we think."

"Property records are public. Right?"

"Good idea. Want to go look at that real quick? I can help you—these new archives are easy to use, but there is so much shit loaded into them."

Tyler stood up and closed his laptop. "Sure, our stuff should be okay to leave here—just put everything in your backpack and push in the chairs."

Danny moved quickly as he did this, leaving the two free to roam the halls toward the state-of-the-art archives section.

Neither of them saw Ella through the window, strolling across campus, headed for the library.

22

He'd sent her a message saying he'd be at the library, and Ella had taken it as an invitation to join them. She wasn't sure how she felt about Tyler and Danny hanging out, considering Danny didn't like her. He knew something. He was suspicious. She sensed it every time they conversed. Now, if she wanted to stay close to Tyler, she'd have to throw Danny off her trail. That was easier said than done, however, since she knew those who were suspicious by nature never really trusted anyone. While she could have just killed Danny, that seemed like less of a challenge. Besides—Tyler was her ultimate goal.

She made her way into the front of the library. The stern librarian, Mrs. Saunders, stood behind the checkout desk. When she saw Ella, her eyes narrowed and a smug, superior look slipped onto her face. "Can I help you find something?" It wasn't a friendly question.

Ella had no idea why the librarian always made faces at her when she came in. Perhaps she was jealous of the younger women, or maybe she just didn't like the looks of Ella. She wasn't sure what it was, but it boiled her blood and she immediately thought about killing the woman. Looking around, Ella realized they were the only two at the front of the library. That's when she got an idea. Tyler had always talked about how Mrs. Saunders was so helpful. Maybe to the male students, but Ella suspected that female students weren't so taken with Mrs. Saunders' charm. She wore a string of pearls around her neck and dressed like she worked in an office rather than a library. Ella knew the only place she'd be able to get the woman alone was in the archives, a room that housed some incredibly old books about the old West. "Yes, I am doing a report for my local history class and I was wondering if you might have anything in the archive about the Gold Rush. Firsthand accounts. Journals, stuff like that."

The woman's look softened. Perhaps she had a soft spot for Colorado history. Ella couldn't be sure. But Mrs. Saunders put on a smile and said, "Of course. We have some journals you might find helpful." Then she began rattling off names of people who, presumably, had come to Colorado during the Gold Rush.

Ella smiled and threw on an excited expression. "Those would be perfect. It would be really great to read, firsthand, what they went through. I can't imagine life back then was easy."

This sent Mrs. Saunders into another long explanation as she set out a sign instructing people to check out at the back desk, then came from behind the desk to lead Ella to the archives in the basement. She used her key to open a door, then stepped through. Ella followed.

Ella felt a surge of anger run through her. As they descended the stairs, she took her knife from her pocket and with a foot to the small of the librarian's back, kicked her down the remaining steps. Twenty concrete steps in all.

Mrs. Saunders hit the concrete at the bottom with a sickening thud, then let out a horrific moan. Ella hurried down the steps, lifted the woman's head as she started another groan, and twisted until there was a crunch. Then she let go, unsure exactly what she intended to do with the body. She hadn't thought that far ahead, but the simple act of killing the librarian made her feel a little better. Bending down, she grabbed Mrs. Saunders by her feet and dragged her into a large walk-in maintenance closet. Surely there was something in there she could use to remove the old crone's head. Flicking on the light, her eyes searched the myriad of mops, brooms, and cleaners until she found, nestled under an inconspicuous shelf, a small axe. First, she slipped off her dress, just in case. Then, she positioned the librarian's body so her head hung over a five-gallon cleaning bucket, then carefully used her knife to cut the jugular, hoping to release just enough blood so removing the head wouldn't be a messy affair. Taking off the woman's pearls, she wrapped them in a rag, then set about removing Mrs. Saunders's head. The axe was dull, but after a few swings she was able to separate bone and sinew, and flesh from flesh until the head was free of the body. She lifted it up and looked at it. The head's tongue lolled to one side, the eyes glossy and dead. In a few hours, the corneas would cloud.

Wrapping the head in a trash bag, and grabbing the pearls, she shut the closet door behind her, then took up her dress and backpack and slipped into the downstairs bathroom to clean herself up and get dressed again. She then stuffed the head and pearls in her backpack and slipped back upstairs, turning off lights as she went. Back in the library, she padded over the industrial carpet-lined floors, through the stacks and study areas until she recognized Tyler and Danny's things, unattended, at a remote table. She had no idea when they'd be back, so she worked quickly.

Ella pushed their things aside to clear the center of the table. Removing the head from her backpack and its trash bag, she gingerly set it down. Then, reaching into her bag, she pulled out the pearls and placed them carefully around what remained of the librarian's neck. When she finished with her macabre centerpiece, she shoved the trash bag back into her bag, and slipped through the stacks. On her way out, the same way she'd come in, a book caught her eye. This history of poisons. *This could be handy*, she thought, and slipped the book into her backpack. Then she strode out of the library, into fading daylight and across the walkway between the library and the arts building.

She found a nearby trashcan just outside and threw out the bloody bag and made her way to the opposite building and into the bathroom to wash her hands and make sure there was no stray blood splatter.

Twenty minutes later, she emerged from the other building to find police sirens howling nearby, and uniformed officers entering the library.

"Do you know what's happening?" a passing student asked, fear in her eyes.

Ella debated telling the girl that the serial killer, Amelia Doss, was on the loose, just to relish in the girl's fear, but she knew better. She didn't need Ella's cover blown. Not yet. "No. I just came out of the building and saw all this."

A crowd of students was gathering, and additional police officers arrived. "Did any of you see anything? Maybe someone running out of the library?" one officer asked.

All around her, students shook their heads, and Ella shook her head right along with them.

"Well, you should all get to your classes or go back to your dorms."

"What happened?" a man asked. He looked like a professor.

"We can't say, sir. We just need this crowd to disperse unless you saw something. Like someone leaving the library who looked suspicious, or scared, or maybe they were running?"

Ella turned and started toward the parking lot where her car was. There was really no point in staying on campus. If she stuck around, it might look fishy. So, she hurried to her car and once she was inside, texted Tyler. *Was going to meet you at the library, but there were cops going inside and they were keeping everyone out. Please tell me you're okay!*

She drove home, pleased with herself. But when she arrived, the shadows weren't pleased with her. The night before, she'd gone to bed without really acknowledging them. Pretending to be Ella could be exhausting, hence the reason she was so tempted to stir up her own legend just so their belief in her would grow and feed her, strengthening her.

Now, they huddled around her, watching her drink her nightly tea. "Well? Speak," she commanded.

"Danny," one of them croaked.

"What about him?"

"He was here, lurking around. Going through your things. He took the key. Smelled the rot downstairs," the shadow said, its voice sounding like a hoarse old woman.

"That son-of-a-bitch." She stood. It was tempting to go out even now, slip into Danny's dorm room and slit his throat. However, it was too soon. Besides, if she killed Danny, it was possible the authorities might put Tyler under protection or even surveillance. She could manage digital surveillance just fine since it cut out whenever she or the shadows were around, but she wouldn't be able to hide for too long with many people looking for her. "How do we deal with Danny?" she asked aloud, not really expecting the shadows to answer.

Sitting back down, she picked her tea up and took another sip. "Did he find Betty's remains?"

"No," one shadow said, then giggled.

"Perhaps it's time for me to kill someone Danny would miss."

"Tyler!" several shadows spat in unison.

"Not yet." She flashed a scowl at them. "I need to teach Danny a little lesson. He's had his eyes on the cheerleaders. One in particular." While she didn't know if he was obsessed, she had seen him watching the cheerleaders when they practiced in the grassy area just outside the dorms. His eyes followed them with great interest, pupils dilated when he saw Karen McBride. Ella had partied with Karen a few times, and when they saw one another, they said hello. Sure, it was a casual acquaintance. It would be easy to get Karen to join her for a coffee, then pull her off into some dark nook or cranny and kill her, leaving her outside Danny's window or in his bedroom. Or maybe she would let Karen live just in case she wanted seconds. Just mutilate her. It would require drugging her, though. Her eyes wandered to her backpack near the door. She had taken the book about poisons from the library, thinking it might be fun to poison a few of Tyler's professors. It would keep the police busy at least, looking for seemingly unrelated killers.

But then a snag in her plan came to light. What if they closed the campus due to all the murders? "They wouldn't do that," she assured herself. Denver could be a vile place. Night after night on the local news, the first thing the reporter did was give the daily death count. What were a few more deaths? She drew in a deep breath and looked over at the shadows, her lips pursed. "No, I think it's a good plan," she said, without expounding on it.

"Yes," the shadows hissed, cackling through the house like an infernal choir.

"I still have so much more for Tyler to be afraid of. I want him to be terrified, then lull him into a false sense of security, and then kill him slowly, so he can watch in horror as I rip him apart." Joy and excitement rushed through her.

Her phone buzzed from the coffee table. She leaned forward and grabbed it. It was a text from Tyler: *Bad shit. Librarian dead. Exhausted. Going to bed.*

An unbidden sigh escaped her lips. *That's terrible. Talk later. Sleep well,* she texted back.

She would not get anything out of Tyler now. The nature of the text alone was much more closed off than previous messages. Danny must have said something to cause Tyler to clam up. Or maybe it was just her imagination. "I'm being paranoid, maybe," she told the shadows, then she handed her tea mug to one of them who had taken solid form. "Go get me another cup of tea and bring me the book from my backpack. I have people to poison." Ella smiled and closed her eyes, then opened them again and sat up straight. "Also, make sure all the homeless know my name and make sure they believe in me. Spread my name across the campus as well. Make sure my legend falls into the hands of everyone who can hear you. I need more strength." A sly smile slipped onto her lips. It was going to be a busy week.

$$\approx \quad 23 \quad \approx$$

"Well, that was an epic waste of time," Tyler said, he and Danny leaving the archives empty handed. They had found the public records for the property listed under Amelia's address, but it only provided information from the original builder in the 1950s and her Aunt Betty's basic information. Information Danny already had. Half an hour passed as they continued to dig, coming up empty-handed.

"No time is wasted in the hunt for answers," Danny said. "You never know when you'll strike gold, so you just have to keep digging until something comes up. Trust me, I've had plenty of nights bored out of my mind."

"If you say so, it just seems we could have been doing something else productive."

"Trust the process."

They started back for their table at the other side of the library where they had left their backpacks and computers.

"What is that?" Danny asked once their table came into sight. "We didn't leave anything out, right?"

Tyler squinted for a better look, the object resembling a

small animal with its long, stringy hair splayed across the surface, a pool of red goo spreading from the center. "Is that a dead dog?"

"Kinda looks like it."

"Shit—she's here."

The two looked around before taking another step, the hairs on Tyler's back standing at attention. The library remained rather deserted, their table out of sight from anyone passing by.

"What do we do? Leave?" Danny asked, his tone falling more hushed.

"We can't just leave a dead animal in the middle of the library. We need to at least tell someone. Let's take a closer look—maybe it's just a prank."

Danny looked at him with doubt swimming behind his eyes. They both knew the odds were against it being a prank, but it would be best to make sure, before doing something drastic like alerting the authorities because of a rubber dog and red corn syrup.

They took slow steps toward the table, eyes narrowing on the object. Once they stood ten feet away, Danny's hand shot up to his mouth, smacking himself on the face as he gasped. "That's not a dog—it's a fucking *head*!"

Tyler's heart pounded so hard in his ears that he nearly missed what Danny had said, but he saw for himself, not needing confirmation of what befell his eyes. "Holy shit. It's Mrs. Saunders."

He recognized the pearl necklace that had been invisible from a distance, the sharp white now standing out against the red backdrop of blood. Tyler gulped as he worked around the table, his hands out in front of him as if the head might jump up to bite him. He crossed his feet with cautious steps until stopping to see the face straight on, finding it clear to be the university's head librarian.

Tyler had gotten to know her over the past couple of weeks and his multiple visits to the library. She was a middle-aged woman who had once run the Denver Public Library across town, opting to move to the university so her three children—who were reaching college age—could attend with a generous discounted tuition. She had actually shown Tyler the best hiding spots in the building for true quiet time after a brief discussion of their favorite Dean Koontz books.

Tyler shook his head. "This can't be real."

"It's real, man. Amelia's here, and we need to leave."

Danny pulled out his cell phone and dialed the police, informing them of the head.

"They told us to wait here and to not touch anything," Danny said, begrudgingly stuffing his phone into his pocket. "This is fucked-up, Ty. We have to tell the cops about Amelia —we're the ones in danger now. We need protection until she's caught."

"She's going to grow stronger once we do. This is what she wants. She plants fear and is trying to put us in a situation to say her name aloud, spread it to others to repeat and research. We might need to leave the city."

"And go where?" Danny asked, sirens sounding in the distance. He tossed his hands in the air. "Go back to Ridgeway where she *lives*? That would be suicide."

"So is standing in this library."

Danny cupped his hands around his lips and shouted. "Is anyone here?! Come help!"

They looked around as his voice echoed, bouncing around the shelves of books, footsteps clopping down one of the aisles.

A young woman appeared from behind Tyler, and he spun around to see her shocked face as she saw the head on the table.

"Ohmygod," she murmured, clutching her stomach and

dashing to the nearest trash can, letting her dinner fly from her mouth in dramatic heaves.

"Denver PD!" a deep voice shouted from the library's entrance.

"Back here!" Danny yelled back. "East side of the building!"

They waited as multiple footsteps rumbled the floor, five police officers rounding the corner and coming to a halt when they saw Tyler and Danny.

"Get on the ground!" the officer in front snarled, his gun pointing at Tyler's face.

"Wait, we didn't—" Tyler began, his hands shooting straight up.

"Get the fuck down!"

Tyler's knees gave out, and he lowered himself to the ground as he watched Danny do the same across the table, Mrs. Saunders' lifeless eyes gazing at the ceiling.

The officer rushed Tyler, twisting his arms behind his back and smacking on a pair of cuffs in one swift motion. Within seconds, he had pulled Tyler up to his knees, towering over him with a smug look of satisfaction. They had placed Danny in a similar position.

"Sorry, boys," the officer said, a scruffy bull of a man whose name tag read ANDERSON. "We can't take any chances, not with a second murder on campus—anyone can be a suspect."

"It wasn't us, Officer," Tyler pleaded. "We were just studying here and came back to find this."

More police arrived, several branching out to cover the building, the radio crackling that the rest of the victim's body had been found in a basement room. Officer Anderson lowered his volume. "Bring the friend over here."

A female officer guided Danny next to Tyler, and the two exchanged a frightened look.

"Officer Foster here is going to search you for any weapons and identification," Anderson said, pulling out a notepad. "You boys go to school here, I assume?"

"Yes, sir," Danny said. "Our backpacks are on those chairs. My wallet is inside with my ID." He nodded toward the bloody table.

Anderson nodded and stepped toward it, slipping on a pair of rubber gloves before pulling out the chairs and seizing the backpacks.

"They're clear," Officer Foster said from behind Tyler. "Want me to uncuff them?"

Anderson nodded, pulling out Danny's wallet from his backpack while also taking out the laptop.

Tyler's heart raced at the sight of the computer. All they'd have to do is flip open the screens to find tabs of research on a deranged serial killer, something that would not bode well in their favor.

"Daniel Espinoza from Ridgeway," Anderson said.

"And this is Tyler Reynolds," Foster said, moving to the front of the boys to join Anderson.

"Tyler Reynolds from Ridgeway, also?" he asked, eyebrows shooting up. "Tyler and Danny?"

The officers exchanged a glance, while Tyler and Danny did the same, only theirs were complete puzzlement.

"Yes, Officer," Tyler said. "I'm sorry, but why do you sound like you know who we are?"

"Funny enough, I've been in contact with Sheriff Abbott from Ridgeway. The last four murders on campus are still cold cases, so we've been looking into anyone tied to the victims." He motioned to Tyler. "You two were obviously at the top of our list since Tyler was the roommate of one of them, and Danny here is the one who found the body first. We did some digging, found out about your other friend who was murdered in Ridgeway during your senior year of high school. Sorry to hear that, boys. All that aside, I reached out to the sheriff, and he filled me on the happenings in Ridgeway —sounds like quite the mess."

"Wait, there have been other murders here on campus?" Danny asked.

"Mrs. Casey from the cafeteria, one of the groundskeepers, and the football coach, Mr. Ellington. Mrs. Casey, we're still not sure about. The groundskeeper, we have no suspects but think that may have been a transient. The coach, we suspect the wife. He was cheating on her with everything in a skirt." He let out an exasperated sigh. "Your sheriff suggested to me I had Ridgeway's serial killer here in Denver now."

"So . . . you know about Amelia?" Danny asked, hesitant.

Anderson looked around, his lips pursed. "Foster, I'm gonna take these boys into a private room for further questioning. You okay out here?"

"Yes, sir, I'll secure the perimeter."

Anderson nodded and turned. "Let's go."

Even with the library swarming with dozens of police officers, a certain calm had settled over Tyler, just knowing they were safe. For now, at least. They followed Officer Anderson through an aisle of bookshelves, crossing the library until reaching the row of conference rooms. He peeked into the first one and let himself in.

The room was deserted, two rectangular tables with an end cap to form a U-shape filling the space. A window provided an unobstructed view of the western side of campus, Tyler able to see his dorm building across the way.

Anderson paced toward the window and lifted his foot onto the ledge, stretching his hamstrings. "Look, boys, I don't know what kind of business you nice folks get into out in the mountains, but I don't think we would ever entertain the idea of a serial killer coming back from the dead. We see too much shit in the city to chalk anything up to superstition. Sheriff

Abbott sounded like a nice enough guy, but I'm sure he doesn't deal with murders on a regular basis. We find a body maybe once a week down here, some are murders, others are bums left out to die like stray animals. We have the bad guys, and we usually catch them." Anderson paused and returned his foot to the floor, pivoting around and crossing his arms as he faced the boys. "I'd be lying if I told you this hasn't caught my attention, but tell me, why should I believe a word of it?"

Anderson's eyes danced back and forth, waiting for one of them to speak up. Tyler knew Danny would, so bit his lip and waited.

"Because she's real, Officer," Danny finally said. "We didn't believe it, either, but we saw her with our own eyes. *Survived* her attacks. It doesn't matter if you believe in her—she's out there, and she'll kill again."

Tyler wondered if it would benefit them to tell Anderson about Danny's findings at Ella's house, but they were both feeling out the officer, trying to gauge if they could trust him or not. So far, it was a mixed bag for Tyler.

"She's after us," Tyler said. "We think that since we got away from her in Ridgeway, she's not stopping until we're dead. Our ancestors have a not-so-great history, and I think she's been out to get me since the beginning. We didn't think she'd have any way of following us to Denver, but these murders all look like they were done by her."

"So you boys have been playing at detective?" Anderson asked, smirking.

"We understand most law enforcement won't take this matter seriously," Danny said. "So we've had to look out for ourselves. If we hadn't, we'd both be dead by now."

Anderson studied them, his eyes beaming into each of them like lasers. "Okay, we obviously can't pursue much without any evidence. I'll reach back out to Sheriff Abbott and see if he can share anything that might align with these murders. If we find something, I'll take a closer look into this whole Amelia Doss matter, but until then, I have to follow the evidence that we have."

"She eats people," Tyler said. "It's how she feeds herself. And not in some private, cannibalistic way with seasoning and cooking, she bites the flesh right off of people, dead or alive. We've read about the dead homeless population, we saw about the ripped flesh that everyone thinks was animals—it's not. It's Amelia, and we really need you to see that."

Tyler felt the early stages of rage boiling within, frustrated that they were starting at square one in a new city. He understood Amelia was a tricky situation for objective people like police officers and detectives to comprehend, but why did every one of them seem so completely closed-minded about the matter?

"You also need to keep it to yourself," Danny said, somewhat snide.

"Excuse me?!" Anderson snapped.

Tyler raised his hands. "He doesn't mean it like that. Amelia gains strength with the more people who believe in her. I guess it feeds her soul, you could say. We want you to believe this, but you can't spread the word beyond yourself, if possible. If the entire Denver Police Department found out, Amelia could become unstoppable."

Anderson furrowed his brow, his own frustrations clearly shining through his hard demeanor. "Okay, I'm going back out there to help my team. I need to sleep on this and make some inquiries. We'll be in touch."

He reached into his inside coat pocket and pulled out two business cards, passing one to each of them.

"Thank you, Officer," Tyler said, forcing a soft grin.

"You two try to stay on campus and be safe, and don't go off half-cocked trying to do a detective's work. Leave that to the professionals."

Anderson swiveled around and stepped out of the conference room, not bothering to wait for the boys to follow.

"Well, this is getting interesting," Tyler said, offering a light, nervous chuckle.

"Let's get out of here."

They left the conference room, both of them sensing, but not acknowledging a looming showdown against Amelia Doss.

❧ 24 ❧

When the phone rang, Danny practically jumped out of his skin. He didn't know what he was expecting. Perhaps Amelia Doss would jump out of his closet or burst through the dorm door. Ever since he and Tyler found Mrs. Saunders' head in the library, it had been painfully clear that Amelia Doss knew where they were. Before, it was just an unfounded suspicion. Knowing it for a fact was an entirely different matter. He picked up his phone, recognized it as a number likely from Ridgeway, and answered. "Hello?"

"Mr. Espinoza. Danny. It's Sheriff Abbott up in Ridgeway."

Danny's stomach twisted a bit. Were his parents okay? "Hey, Sheriff. Is everything okay?" There was no way to hide the worry in his voice.

"Well, you tell me, son. I had a call from that Detective Anderson. Or is it Officer? Regardless, he told me about what happened with the librarian and some of the additional murders that you guys seem to think are related to Amelia. I actually tried to get ahold of Tyler's parents, but they're out tonight, and I didn't have Tyler's number, so I called your parents to get your number instead." Sheriff Abbott went quiet for a second, waiting for a response.

"Yeah," Danny started. "We're positive at this point it's Amelia Doss, sheriff. The Denver Police don't believe us, naturally."

"I can't say I blame them. Son, you know how hard it was for me to believe we had a supernatural serial killer on the loose? You don't shoot a person at close range like that, in the spot I hit her, without them dropping and bleeding out." The sheriff went quiet for a moment, and Danny knew it was because he was probably remembering the whole incident. You didn't live through something like that without some emotional scarring, and it seemed Sheriff Abbott hadn't escaped unscathed either.

"So how do we convince the police here?"

"Can you? As far as they know, they're experiencing a rash of murders all over the campus. What, there was the football coach, a groundskeeper, cafeteria worker, and now the librarian? Plus Tyler's roommate. That's five." Sheriff Abbott drew in a deep breath. "Possibly others off-campus. I've read about the murders within the homeless population. But how many of them are related?"

Danny didn't offer an answer to the hypothetical question, because he had no way of knowing. What he knew was that he and Tyler were in danger. "Even if we chalked up all the murders as coincidence and a streak of violence—Mrs. Saunders, the librarian, her head was left specifically for me and Tyler. And... I don't know if you heard about this or not, but Tyler found Bryson Day's letterman jacket in his closet and he's been getting emails from an anonymous address."

"Bryson's grave was dug up. The body is still missing. Why didn't you kids call me the second that jacket showed up?"

Danny faltered for a second. The sheriff was right. Why hadn't they? "I . . . I don't know."

"I agree, it sounds like she's back, but how is that even possible? How did she get to Denver? Where is she living?" The sheriff went quiet again, and Danny could envision that look of consternation Sheriff Abbott always got when he was thinking something through. "Do you need me to come out there?"

"The local police are on it, Sheriff."

"Yeah, but it's unlikely they're going to believe you're dealing with a dead serial killer. A wraith or something." Clearly Sheriff Abbott had been having the same thoughts as Danny about Amelia Doss.

"Demon, actually. I talked to some local witches and they've given me a good idea of a ritual we need to complete to put her back in the grave once and for all. We just need to find time to come back up to Ridgeway to do it. It has to be done over her grave," Danny explained. He'd already put together the ritual in his head based on the books the witches had recommended, he just wasn't sure of himself. He'd been thinking of heading back to Dark Works in order to run it by the women there and see if they had any advice. If there was time, of course.

"Demon?"

"Well, it makes sense. See, she's not a vampire even though she eats human flesh and feeds off people's belief in her."

The sheriff chuckled. "Sounds like a damn vampire to me."

"Well, she would only drink blood. Not eat flesh. Flesh-eating is for zombies," Danny explained. "But, the point being the women at the witchcraft shop thought that maybe we were dealing with a demon, or a devil rather. Because someone who is evil in life can become a devil in death."

"What's the difference between a devil and a demon?"

"Semantics, the century you're living in, and the religion you come from, apparently," he said, laughing a little to himself. "She's evil, though—I think we can both agree on that."

"You and Tyler be careful, and if you need me, call me. You'll do that, right?" There was a grave edge to the sheriff's voice.

"We will, sir. Thank you for reaching out, and I'll let Tyler know you called," he said. They hung up and Danny was left standing there, deep in thought. He needed to talk to Tyler. Grabbing his coat and keys, he left his dorm room and headed to Tyler's, remembering the protection amulet in his desk drawer. He hadn't been wearing it, but was wondering if he should. The short distance from his building to Tyler's required him to go outside, and it was dark. He sprinted the distance. Something about being outside made him feel vulnerable, and how that was going to play out when he had to work at night, he didn't know. He only relaxed once he got into the building and halfway up the flight of stairs leading to Tyler's.

Tyler's room was completely tidy when Danny got there. Even the floor had been swept. The area rugs were perfectly symmetrical, and it appeared he had dusted all the flat surfaces.

"Doing a little cleaning?"

"Nervous energy, you know?" Tyler asked, putting the chain on the door. "We knew she was here because of the jacket."

Danny knew exactly what he meant. The head of the librarian made the danger they were in feel more tangible. "I got a call from Sheriff Abbott."

Tyler pursed his lips together. "And?"

"And he told us to be careful. He offered to come out if we needed him to."

"So he could do what? Shoot her a few more times? It didn't stop her before." Tyler sat down on the edge of his neatly made bed. "Besides, we don't even know where to find her!"

"I still think Ella is the connection," Danny said, knowing damn well he was opening a can of worms by the mere utterance of Ella's name.

Tyler rolled his eyes.

"She doesn't have a traceable past. Her school hasn't heard of her. She probably got into college on a false application. There's no sign of her aunt. There was a stink in the basement. She didn't start college until she was twenty-one. You don't find any of that strange?" He couldn't keep the exasperation from his voice. Why couldn't Tyler see what Danny saw as red flags everywhere?

"There could be a hundred and one reasons for all of that. Maybe her parents are dead and she doesn't want to talk about it? Or maybe they had some huge falling out. Maybe it just took her time to save enough money to come to school. Maybe her aunt really is in Michigan, like she said. And maybe what you smelled in the basement was a dead animal that crawled under the house or something. Or a dead mouse. I'm sure there's a logical explanation."

Danny gave him a paranoid look and crossed his arms over his chest. He knew if he pushed it too much further, they'd be fighting again. "Fine, we need to concentrate on Amelia Doss. So I went to a few local witchcraft shops and one of them had some good information. We have to do the ritual on a full moon."

"Why a full moon?"

"I don't know. It's just this is working with necromancy and the moon gives it more power." Danny pulled out the desk chair and sat down. "We will have to go back to Ridge-way, to her grave, and do the ritual over it." A chill swept up his body, and he involuntarily shuddered.

"What if she follows us?"

"Then she follows us. There will be certain protections in place," he lied. Well, he'd give Tyler the amulet, but Danny was going to be a sitting duck.

"What makes you so sure you can do it? It's not like you're a witch or something, unless you've been keeping it from me." A small smirk appeared on Tyler's lips.

"I was the one who raised her from the dead, wasn't I? I was able to do that, so I should be able to put her back into the ground." Danny wrung his hands together, then let out the breath he'd been holding. "It's our only chance to get rid of her once and for all."

"All right," Tyler finally said. "It's not like we have any other plans. She's too strong for us to physically fight her and impervious to bullets, so..."

"Good," Danny said, an awkward span of silence slowly building.

"How do we know if it works?" Tyler asked.

It was a legitimate question, one Danny had asked himself a thousand times. "We just have to wait and see."

"Wait and see if anyone else is murdered?"

"Yeah." Danny swallowed, his throat dry.

"Great."

"Well, it's not like..." Then he had an idea. "We can have the witches do a divination for us."

"What if it doesn't work?" Tyler lifted his eyebrows in question.

This time, Danny shrugged. "We go to the witches and see if they can help us."

"So either way, witches?" He let out a nervous laugh.

"It's our plan B." Biting his upper lip, Danny stood. "So I

should get going. I am working an early shift in the morning. Covering a few hours for a friend before classes."

Tyler nodded.

"Tyler, please just be careful of Ella. I'm not saying she's willingly part of Amelia Doss's plan to hurt you, but there's something not right about her. Things about her past..." He left it hanging in the air.

"I still think you're being paranoid, but if it helps, I'll confront Ella about her past. Okay? See if I can get more information." Then a thoughtful look passed over his face. "And I'll be careful."

"Thanks, man. That's all I ask." Then Danny left. He looked at his watch. It was a bit late, but he wondered if he could get one of the witches from Dark Works on the phone. He pulled the phone out of his pocket and dialed the number just as he stepped outside of Tyler's dorm hall and started toward his own. Much to his surprise, a woman answered.

"Dark Works. This is Lavinia."

"Hi, my name is Danny Espinoza, and I was in the other day asking about devils."

"Skinny college guy, spiky black hair?"

"Yeah." He chuckled. "I am going to do a ritual to get rid of my devil during the full moon."

"Good time to do it," she said. "The moon lends significant power to magic."

"I have a question though—how will I know if it works?" He cringed at the thought.

"Oh, you'll know if it works. You'll see the spirit sucked into the pit," she said, her voice taking on a foreboding tone.

"Even if the spirit isn't there?"

"Time and space have no meaning in the spirit world. When you do the ritual it will open a rift that draws the spirit in and sends them back to whence they came."

Whence they came. It was an awkward expression. "And if she comes back again?"

"Danny, if that spirit comes back again, you're probably going to have to seek a full-blown exorcism to get rid of this devil."

"Do you know anyone who can do that?" Just as he asked, he saw a black shadow out of his right eye, rushing through the trees on the grassy area across from his dorm building's entrance. Quickening his pace, he hurried inside.

"My coven will gladly help you out if you aren't able to get rid of the spirit itself. Are you okay? You sound a bit out of breath."

"I'm fine. I just thought I saw something, but... it was nothing." He paused in the lobby, his eyes looking through the window in the direction he saw the black figure. It had only been a fleeting shadow.

"Put on that amulet you bought," she suggested.

"I'll do that as soon as I get upstairs to my room," he said, and turned toward the hallway leading to his place.

"Good. If you have any more problems, let me know, okay?" Lavinia sounded genuinely concerned, and that put Danny at ease.

"Thank you. I really appreciate it and I hope I didn't call too late."

"It's not a problem, Danny. Talk soon!"

"Thanks, Lavinia. Goodnight." He hung up feeling more confident.

Outside, in the dark spaces between the bushes across from the dorm buildings, the shadows watched.

❧ 25 ❧

Ella had always hated girls like Karen McBride. While they didn't have cheerleaders in Ridgeway in the 1920's, there was no shortage of women like her. They were women who knew how pretty they were, who flaunted it, and who looked down their noses at other women. Despite this, Ella had become friends with a few of the cheerleaders during parties. They were clean and their flesh smelled sweet and tender. Because Ella was so popular, the cheerleaders were kind to her and said hello whenever they passed. She also realized that perhaps she'd been killing the wrong people. If she expected people to fear the name Amelia Doss, she needed a higher profile. Instead of killing inconspicuous librarians and groundskeepers, or resented coaches, perhaps it was time to butcher one of the campus darlings.

Now, Karen McBride stood in line to pay for her salad. Ella watched her, nursing a rare hamburger that was a little overcooked for her tastes. However, if she wanted to appear human, she had to be seen eating human food and rare burgers were the only thing she could partly stomach. That and water and tea. Anything else and she'd find herself in the bathroom throwing up. How desperately she craved fresh, young meat, and Karen's calf and thigh muscles looked decadent. Her mouth watered.

When Karen finished paying, she turned towards the tables, her eyes searching for a friendly face. Ella raised her hand, caught her attention, and motioned her over.

Karen threw on a big smile and started toward her, her short cheer skirt bouncing as she walked. She got to the table and set her tray down, then sat. "Hey Ella! Girl, we have some serious partying to do."

"We do?" Ella forced a smile.

"Costume party at Todd's tonight. Beer bongs, shots, live band. And there will be edibles there. You just have to go with a friend, make sure you don't get roofies in your drink. You should pick an awesome costume." She picked up her fork and stabbed at the lettuce, shoving a goodly amount into her maw.

"Sounds like fun. I'm in," she said, realizing she'd have to look up "roofies".

"My friend, Liz, got roofied once. But luckily, our other friend, Margot, was there with her and fended off the guy, then took her home. It was some band geek trying to get laid. So fucked-up," she said, taking another bite of her salad.

"I thought roofies…" but she didn't get the sentence out of her mouth.

Karen nodded with vigor. "Right? I guess the dose was small enough she could still walk. It just makes you compliant. A high enough dose, though, could actually knock a person out."

"What's the address?" Ella asked, pulling out a small notebook.

The cheerleader gave it to her in between bites of salad, then started talking about her quarterback boyfriend. Ella didn't care, but she smiled and acted interested, anyway. "You should take an Uber or something so you can drink. No drinking and driving," she said in a sing-song voice.

"Oh, of course not," Ella said. While alcohol loosened some of her inhibitions, it also made her really hungry. She'd left the last two parties starving, which led her to a few of the homeless encampments over by the train tracks. The homeless were already whispering Amelia Doss. While most people figured they were crazy and didn't listen, there were enough mentally ill in the city that word was spreading and the legend of Amelia Doss in Denver, while in its infancy, was growing. She could feel it in her bones, and she'd felt more rested—stronger.

Karen continued on about her classes and her friends, and a dress she bought. Not once did she ask Ella about her life, her dresses, or her friends. *Not surprising*, she thought. Finally, the young woman finished her lunch and got up. "Well, I have to get to biology for another annoyingly long lecture. See you tonight, Ella!" Then she pranced off and flirted with a few guys as she left.

At least Ella was alone with her thoughts now. She hadn't had time to find or brew any poisons to kill Tyler's professors, but she might have time to find something to drug Karen with. Perhaps even these roofies Karen talked about. Wouldn't it be funny if Karen went along willingly? She giggled to herself, then gathered her things and left the cafeteria, deciding to ditch her classes for the rest of the day in search of the perfect costume, and the perfect drug for Karen.

SHE PICKED UP A COSTUME FROM A LOCAL PARTY STORE ON the way home, then tasked her shadow friends to find the roofies—which weren't hard to procure. By seven-thirty, after the sun had set, the shadows found a local dealer and led Ella right to him. When he asked for money, she simply slit his throat and left him to bleed out. No one would care that the world was short one dealer who'd died under a bridge while practicing his trade. Ella and the shadows returned home where she changed her clothes. Her dark friends were coming with her tonight. Well, they always came, but they often stayed outside. Tonight, however, they'd come inside. There were plenty of tenebrous places for them to hide. In closets and cupboards, rooms and stairwells. She didn't care either way. The shadows could do the heavy lifting if necessary. As she got ready, an urgency overcame her. She knew that the time to dispatch Tyler was drawing nearer. Drawing out this tedious life of popularity and parties wouldn't change that. No, she decided. She was going to do it and she would have to do it in the coming week. Then, and only then, would she be able to rest.

The shadows could feel how weary she was, and they watched her closely. "Amelia," they whispered as she emerged from the bathroom in a fresh, long black skirt. It hadn't snowed yet, and Halloween was just around the corner. She put on the reaper mask and long, cowl hooded cloak. One of the shadows handed her the plastic scythe.

In her skirt pocket, she had her key, student ID, her knife, and the baggie of roofies. What else could she have possibly needed? "I need fresh meat, and I need more people to speak my name," she said.

"Don't kill her. Just eat her and maim her. Let her live in case you want seconds," one shadow said with a hearty laugh.

Ella looked at it with an amused grin. "Not a bad suggestion, my friend."

A few of the shadows began bouncing with excitement. "The time draws near."

"It does. Both for the party and for Tyler." She glanced at her cell phone and noticed her ride was on the way. Uber was one of those things she learned about from Rachelle and her other college friends.

Cackles filled the house, and Ella threw back her head and laughed with them. It was almost a relief. Once they'd had their fill of merriment, and the Uber arrived, Ella and a few of the shadows slipped out of the house and headed to the party.

Karen had been right. The early arrivals were all attractive men and women. They were the who's who of campus, so of course, Karen was among them. And now Ella. It was like being invited into a secret society. A vapid secret society, but secret nonetheless.

"Wow, Ella, dark costume," Todd said. He was dressed as the forest god, Pan.

Ella took down her hood. "It *is* Halloween. The season of death. Who better to attend than the Grim Reaper?"

"Yeah, if The Reaper was hot and a woman," some guy said from behind her.

She shot him an amused smile, then glanced over the women present, who were all dressed as something sexy. A sexy cat. A sexy demon. A sexy rabbit. A sexy nurse. "Maybe I could use a drink."

"That's the spirit!" Todd led her into the kitchen and gave her something he called a Hard Lemonade.

Ella enjoyed it and sat back in a corner, one of the shadows with her, and listened to the idle gossip and tall tales of college students whose biggest concern was whether they were going to pass their anthropology and English courses. Slowly, over the next few hours, more and more party-goers arrived, two of them also dressed as the reaper but both men. This was good news because once Karen had the drugs in her system, she wouldn't know who was beneath the cloak, and wouldn't suspect Ella. Despite this, caution was required. Ella rather enjoyed her quiet little house and didn't want to have to hide in the shadows or find a new base camp until she killed Tyler. *Maybe I* should *kill her*, she thought.

"No, Amelia," the shadow behind her whispered. "They need to know Amelia Doss lives and that they must fear her."

The shadow had a point. The more her name was spoken, the more strength she would have to kill Tyler.

"Very well," she said aloud, watching the shadows slip into conversations in dark corners, whispering her name. Sure, many of the students would not hear the shadows outright, but they would hear it in their sub-consciences. It was a seed that, once planted, would grow quickly. Then, when they heard the name *Amelia Doss*, terror would grip them, and they would believe, and Ella would feed.

She waited until she found Karen alone in the kitchen before she approached her. Karen looked like she'd been crying. "Hey, everything okay?" Ella asked, putting a comforting arm around her shoulders.

Karen nodded. "I had a fight with my boyfriend. He left."

"Well, his loss," Ella said, just repeating what she'd heard other young women say to their friends whenever they had a messy breakup.

She nodded. "Yeah. You're right. I could totally have *any* guy at this party."

"You totally could," Ella said, taking out another hard lemonade. This time she slipped two of the roofies into it. Then she mixed it around. "You want one of these?"

Karen nodded and wiped her eyes. She was dressed as Cleopatra and her eye makeup was running. "Yeah, thanks." She took the drink from Ella's grasp and gulped down half of it. "Something about being upset makes me thirsty. Or maybe I just want to get drunk and forget that asshole."

"Good idea," Ella said. She sipped on the dark beer she'd just opened. "What about Todd?"

A laugh erupted from Karen. "Todd's kind of a dork. But this is his place."

"He owns it?"

"No, he rents it. Might not be bad to have a boyfriend off-campus." She finished her drink and handed the empty bottle to Ella, who searched for any sign of the pills. There was nothing.

Ella narrowed her eyes, noting what a state Karen was in. She had no idea how long it took for the pills to kick in. "There's a quiet bathroom in the basement where you could touch up your makeup."

"Great idea." She pointed to the hard lemonades. "Grab me another one of those."

Ella did as instructed and handed it over.

"I'll be back in a few minutes." Then Karen disappeared through the dark hallway and down the stairs. The shadows followed her.

She waited for five minutes, then, with knife in hand, Ella followed.

Ella found Karen slumped on the floor in the bathroom, babbling incoherently. Surprisingly, there was no one else down there, so she slipped off her cloak and into the bathroom, closing and locking the door behind them. Then she lifted Karen and put her in the bathtub. Karen passed out.

"It will make easy work of it," one of the shadows whispered.

Ella nodded. "Yes." Then she sawed off the fingers of Karen's left hand. She took Karen's right eye next, leaving the left one. Then she took a pound of meat from the cheerleader's left thigh and calf, careful to not hit the arteries. She even tied tourniquets above the wounds. She handed the thigh steak and the fingers to one of the shadows. "Get rid of the fingers and freeze this meat at home. I'll eat this calf here."

Leaning over the sink, Ella ate the cheerleader's calf muscle, enjoying the tender, fragrant meat.

The cheerleader stirred. "Amelia Doss did this to you, girl," Ella told her in her regular voice, filled with malice.

"Amelia Doss," the still unconscious girl murmured.

Ella cleaned herself and her knife, donned her cape, and slipped back up to the party with no one realizing she had left.

It took another hour for someone to find Karen McBride. She was still alive. By the time the ambulance arrived and all the underaged drinkers had dispersed, Karen was awake, screaming in pain and telling everyone who would listen that it was Amelia Doss who had done this to her.

The power within Amelia surged. They all knew her name.

✣ 26 ✣

Danny had agreed that Tyler should continue to act normal around Ella. She had never posed a threat to either of them, and Tyler argued it was possible that whatever Danny had smelled in Ella's basement had a logical explanation behind it. They were both on edge, and that could always lead to erratic thinking.

Tyler still felt an attraction he couldn't ignore, thinking about Ella in his free time where his thoughts drifted toward what life could be like if she was his girlfriend. He had sent her a message before his lunch break, asking if she would like to meet. She agreed to join him in the Tivoli building for a slice of pizza.

When Tyler arrived, he fought through the crowded student center, finding Ella sitting along the outer wall away from the ruckus, two plates with a giant slice of pizza on each. The usual smells of baked dough and grilled meat filled the air, the distant sizzle of a grill mixing with the steady hum of conversation. He grinned as he approached her, suddenly forgetting all the worries that had been pent up over the past couple of days.

"Hey, how are you doing?" Tyler asked, pulling out the seat opposite Ella and dropping his backpack on the floor. "Been awhile."

She smiled and nodded. "It has. I've been good. Stuck with this lovely class schedule. How have you been?"

"I take it you heard about the murder in the library?"

"Yes, who hasn't? Place has been closed ever since."

"Well, me and Danny were there . . . we were the first ones to find the body."

Ella didn't offer any sort of reaction, only staring blankly at Tyler. Her eyes bounced from the pizza in front of her to Tyler in a quick motion. "I'm sorry to hear that. Are you guys okay?"

No reaction in her voice, Tyler thought, figuring she had already been numbed from the trauma of losing Jason.

"We've been okay. Don't think it's an image I'll ever be able to shake from my mind. But we'll see."

"Any more offers from the Dean to skip the rest of the year?" Ella asked with a coy grin.

"The offer stands for the rest of the semester, but why stop now? We only have a few more weeks left."

Ella took a bite of pizza, raising it high to catch the droopy cheese trying to fall off the edge of the plate.

Tyler leaned back. "I need to talk to you about something, and I hope you don't take any of this the wrong way."

Ella put her slice down and leaned forward, clasping her hands below her chin. "Okay?"

Tyler felt his legs bounce under the table and whipped his hands down to stop them. "All these murders that have been happening around campus . . . I think they might be tied to me somehow."

Ella furrowed her brow in confusion, eyes beaming into Tyler. "I don't understand."

"Hear me out. There were a series of murders back in my

hometown earlier this year. To make a long story short, we believe the killer was out to get me."

"Who is *we?*"

"Me and Danny—he's been helping me figure this out ever since those first murders in Ridgeway." Tyler had to choose his words carefully, not wanting to mention Amelia by name, in case there was some longshot connection between her and Ella. "That's all beside the point. We think these recent murders have a connection to the Ridgeway ones. Danny and I have done a ton of research, and something we've done to keep ourselves safe is look into people of interest."

Ella continued her gaze absent of emotion, Tyler realizing he'd need to lay everything out in detail. She cocked her eyebrows to tell him to keep going.

"I guess what I'm asking is why we can't find any sort of history for you."

"*Me?!* What did I do?" she asked, somehow still void of emotion.

"Nothing. I said we just look into people. Obviously you were Jason's girlfriend, so you had a connection to his death. Trust me, this is more paranoia on our part than suspicion against anyone. We just want to make sure our tracks are always covered regarding who we deal with daily. We've looked up the backgrounds of several professors as well—you never know."

This was a lie, but Tyler felt he pulled it off as a believable cover story for their snooping around. Ella pursed her lips as she studied Tyler, surely trying to get a feel for this whole situation that had just been dumped onto her lap.

"Tell me what you found—I'm curious." She leaned back and crossed her arms, signaling she wouldn't accept anything else.

"Okay. Your social media accounts are all new. That doesn't mean anything, but it is strange for someone our age.

We traced back your parents' names and nothing came up. Same thing with your high school—it all seemed made up, if you don't mind me saying. And that's all we could find. You are virtually off the grid."

Ella nodded, satisfied. "I'm impressed. Everything has held up as we expected."

Now was Tyler's turn to stare across the table, confusion dripping from his face. "I hope you'll explain."

"Of course. You've already gone through this much trouble, the least I can do is put your mind at ease. My family is in a witness protection program. We saw a murder unfold at our next door neighbor's house, and we needed sanctuary after they let the killer off with manslaughter. This all started before he was to be released from prison. So we did the whole thing of changing our names and moving across the country, starting a new life. I won't share my real name or my parents', but they currently live in California and agreed I could come to school out here."

"Huh," Tyler said. "I'd have never guessed."

"You're not supposed to—that's the point."

"So your story about Wyoming and religious parents?"

She gave him a small smile. "Made up."

"Your aunt?"

"A lady I'm renting a room from who agreed to act as my alleged aunt. It was cheaper to rent a room than a dorm room. Plus, I have my own space this way. An entire house to myself at the moment." She shrugged.

Tyler chuckled, immediately relieved by the news. Ella had no history because she wasn't supposed to. "Well, I feel like an idiot now. I'm sorry if I made you feel weird about all of that. Maybe I'm the one who's going crazy, after all."

Ella let out a gentle laugh. "It's fine, no need to apologize. I wouldn't normally share this rather huge detail about my life, but I trust you. I'd hate to see you worried about anything."

Her tone came out caring, almost matronly, and made Tyler's stomach churn with affection. "So where do we go from here? It seems like everything is out in the open now. Do we just pretend that none of this happened and continue with life as it's been?"

Ella shrugged. "I don't think we can brush this under the rug. You know my biggest secret—not even Jason knew this about me." Hearing this made Tyler's heart beat uncomfortably fast. A window of opportunity had just opened, at least through his eyes, and if there was ever a time to ask Ella on a date, it had to be during this conversation. "What do *you* think we should do?"

Tyler's palms moistened with sweat, his legs bouncing again. Ella put the onus on him. He shrugged, thousands of thoughts flooding his mind, his instinct to find a way out of this confrontation kicking in. "I think we should see where things take us."

The word left his lips, and he watched them fall on Ella's ears, waiting to see how she'd react. "Us? I didn't realize there was an *us*." She said this with a smirk, swirling more confusion for Tyler, who now felt cornered by his own conversation. There was no backing out now. He either had to secure a date, or plan to never speak to Ella again.

"Well, I didn't mean it like that. We're friends. We have a special bond over Jason. You know?"

"I'm done with the games, Tyler. I've come to terms with Jason's death. We don't have to play nice anymore. So why don't you tell me what you really want?"

Tyler's face prickled with hot blood, and he thought he might vomit thanks to his gut flipping like a pissed off dolphin. The bounce in his legs made its way into his arms, shaking them with nerves in a way he hadn't experienced since playing youth baseball. Stepping into the batter's box had always brought a powerful wave of anxiety, all eyes on him, waiting to see what he could make happen. This situation with Ella was no different. Her eyes on him, waiting to see what he'd do.

"I want to date you," he said, feeling relief and regret intertwined.

Her smirk widened to a grin. "I thought you might say that. You're a good guy, Tyler, and you stay true to yourself. That's rare these days, especially in college."

She had yet to address his comment, so Tyler braced himself for the inevitable rejection. He had never put himself on the line, finding it unbearably frightening, yet somehow arousing.

"I like you," he said. "There's not much else to it. I've gotten to know you since we've been spending time together. I like you a lot."

Tyler shook his head, knowing he sounded like a total buffoon fumbling over his words. Ella giggled, and the room spun around Tyler.

"Okay," she said. "I'm interested. Let's go on a date. Did you have anything in mind?"

The response stunned Tyler, slapping him across the face to shake some sense back into his mind. "Uh, well, no."

Ella chuckled. "Let's keep it low-key and simple—intimate. How about dinner in your dorm? You have all that extra space now."

"Okay. Tonight?"

Ella shook her head. "I have some things going on tonight. Tomorrow night works for me, though."

Tyler looked toward the ceiling, pretending to check his mental calendar, knowing damn well he had nothing planned and would absolutely be free for a date with his crush. "Tomorrow should work."

"Perfect—it's a date. I'll come over around five, and we'll decide what to eat."

Tyler nodded, a dreamlike sensation still swooning over him. Surely any minute he'd be waking up to realize it was all a dream. *Play it cool. She said yes. No need to be an idiot anymore.*

"Yep, that works for me."

"Great," Ella said, standing up and tossing her empty plate in the trash can next to their table. "I'll see you then. And maybe I'll bring dessert for after we're done eating." She batted her eyes, and Tyler's throat clenched shut, leaving him to nod like a speechless bobblehead doll. She rounded the table and brushed a hand across Tyler's back. "See you tomorrow night."

She walked away, leaving Tyler to deflate in his seat, the tension fleeing as soon as he was alone. "Holy shit," he whispered under his breath, laughing at himself. *Did that really just happen? And what the hell does she mean by 'dessert'?*

Tyler knew damn well what she meant, and the thought brought on a fresh wave of anxiety. He had a date on the calendar, but now had to confront the reality that he might also lose his virginity tomorrow. Everything had progressed so quickly once he stepped into the Tivoli building, and he struggled to make sense of it all. He wanted to tell Danny, but didn't know if admitting to a date with Ella—in his dorm, nonetheless—would stir another disagreement. They had agreed for Tyler to keep a line of communication open with Ella, but was this going too far?

It doesn't matter. She told you the truth—that's what you need to tell Danny. Ella is in the clear. She's not a threat like we thought. Whatever she and I decide to do has no bearing on our research into Amelia.

Tyler rose from his seat, the thought of having sex for the first time making his legs wobbly and hollow. He had to lean against the table to keep from falling on his face. "Get it together, man," he told himself, grabbing his backpack off the floor and taking slow steps out of the student center.

He strolled across campus with his head held high, a new confidence in his stride, feeling on top of the world as he returned to his dorm to clean up for his big date tomorrow night.

❃ 27 ❃

The next day, Danny needed to keep his mind occupied. He had grown sick after Tyler sent him a text message letting him know that Ella was going over to his dorm for a date night. Danny cautioned his friend against it, holding back his true urge to unleash a can of fury via text.

Tyler had only responded letting him know everything was fine, that he and Ella had talked through some things, and she was cleared from being a threat to them.

He'll explain later, Danny thought, thinking back to the last message he had received. "What if there isn't a later?"

He didn't care what Tyler thought; Ella couldn't be trusted. He knew what he saw and smelled in her townhouse, and there was no logical explanation. The odor was death; he had no doubt of it.

If he wants to be this reckless, I can't stop him anymore. I can only control myself, and I will get to the bottom of this.

Danny had returned to his dorm after his later classes with hopes of completing homework before the weekend, maybe dabble on his screenplay before calling it a night. But knowing Tyler was a sitting duck in his own dorm distracted him from achieving anything he wanted.

Instead, he opened his laptop and returned to the deep dive into Ella and Amelia's backgrounds, knowing somewhere the connection lurked. He had exhausted everything he could into Ella's made-up history, coming with fake names and locations. The answer would have to lie with Amelia, and one tunnel they had ventured down was Amelia's past—before she was born. All of their research up until now had centered around her life, her childhood, her rampage across Ridgeway, and of course, her dramatic death.

Danny believed the more he could uncover, even if it seemed irrelevant on the surface, the closer he'd get to the answers he desired.

He had records saved on his computer from pictures he had taken at the Ridgeway Library, hundreds of photos that he had yet to review and move to the appropriate folders he had set up to stay organized. In the collection were images from Amelia's family history, but nothing that had seemed relevant in the early stages—and still didn't. But he had nowhere else to turn for new information.

"Thomas William Kraft," Danny whispered, opening the first document that showed an obituary for Amelia's father. "Leaves behind a widow and two daughters—shit, Amelia had a sister?!"

He had never known this, and now had another rabbit hole to fall into, hopefully within the research in front of him. Danny continued reading about Thomas Kraft, learning that he had immigrated to the United States from Ontario, Canada, first finding work in one of the several factories in Chicago where he'd eventually meet his wife, Abigail. The two married, and Thomas went into business with his brothers to form Kraft Foods, doing door-to-door sales of processed cheese in 1903. With two young girls, Thomas decided to uproot their family from the bustle of Chicago and moved them to Ridgeway, Colorado, where his fortune allowed them to be one of the richest families in the small mountain town. Thomas used his money and entrepreneurial spirit to open a new grocery store in the middle of Ridgeway.

By the end of his life, he had a stint on the city council, a failed campaign for mayor, and had become known as one of the most charitable citizens in Ridgeway history. The Kraft family was adored in town and would be until Amelia tarnished anyone who had a connection to her.

Curious, Danny sifted through more of the files in search for information about a sister to Amelia, but nothing ever came up. Thomas's obituary didn't mention any family names, so Danny wanted to try his wife's to see if it shared any more details. He had to sift through plenty of documents and articles about the famous Thomas Kraft, gradually growing disappointed that most of the undiscovered research was about the philanthropist and politician.

After ten minutes he landed on a new section that seemed to center around the famous man's wife, and when he found the obituary, a knot started to twist in his stomach as he read.

"Abigail Stella Kraft, nee. Jones," Danny read. "Jones?"

He didn't even read beyond that first line, a sense of destiny swooning over him. Ella's last name was Jones, and while a connection couldn't be made from that simple fact—Jones being an incredibly common name both then and still today—it opened a door that heightened all of Danny's senses.

He stared at the name, his curiosity about Amelia's sister now vanished. "Abigail Stella Jones," he said, wanting to hear her full maiden name. So many names were scanned over in the midst of his rigorous research, often in his mind for half a second before being pushed aside. Fortunately, he had organized all of his data in a spreadsheet to easily track down any names or terms that might be of interest.

Danny opened the master sheet, loaded with dozens of tabs and typed in *Abigail*. Nothing turned up, so he punched in *Stella,* his heart falling to the bottom of his stomach as it showed one result in his massive database.

"Holy shit," he said, pushing back from the computer as if it might slam shut on his fingers. Stella Jones was the name listed as Ella's mother on her college application. He stared at the screen, trying to make sense of it, needing to understand what it meant. "Stella. Ella. Jones."

He shook his head and clicked through to pull up Ella's application, skimming the document for the name listed for her father. "William Jones. Fuck. Abigail Stella Jones, Thomas William Kraft. . . she used their fucking middle names!"

Danny's fingers shook as they hovered over the keyboard, unsure what exactly to do next. His mind spun with possibilities, trying to piece together the puzzle. He stood up, circling behind his chair, eyes stuck on the computer screen.

"Think, Danny!" he said, hoping the new perspective would shake fresh thoughts loose. "If Ella is using Amelia's parents' middle names as her own, what does that mean? Where is the fucking *connection*?!"

Hot anger—caused by further confusion in this twisted investigation—brimmed at Danny's surface. It seemed as if the truth was staring him straight in the eye, mocking him, teasing like a cat chasing a laser up a wall.

He needed to take a step back, convinced he was over-thinking everything. His brain had become polluted with every imaginable bit of information about Amelia Doss. "Keep it simple. We have Amelia Doss, maiden name Kraft. Ella Jones. Thomas William Kraft. Abigail Stella Kraft, maiden name Jones."

Danny returned to his seat and pulled a blank piece of

paper out of his desk drawer, pushing his laptop back to clear space and write the names in a list. "Stella. Ella. Stella. Ella."

He circled those two names, staring, calculating, fighting to get his thoughts under control. He crossed out *Kraft*, deeming it irrelevant to the brewing storm. "Abigail Stella Jones." He crossed out *Abigail*. "Stella Jones."

All other words on the paper fell out of his vision, Stella Jones remaining the only relevant name he wanted to look at. *You know what it is—stop lying to yourself. Drop the first two letters of the name and you'll no longer be able to deny your eyes.*

Danny stuck out his index finger and hesitantly slid it across the paper, stopping when it covered the S and T from Stella. "Ella Jones," he whispered, that same finger starting to shake. His mouth flooded with saliva that he needed to gulp, every hair on his back and neck stiff with fear. "Ella Jones is Amelia Doss. Amelia Doss is Ella Jones."

He drew a deep breath, eyes narrowed on Stella Jones as he rummaged through his thoughts in search of any other explanation. If Amelia had a true accomplice, she wouldn't have needed to come up with a fake name. Amelia had limited knowledge of the world and people of current times, leaving her little to choose from when creating her alias. Her husband or kids would have been too obvious, but she showed creativity in structuring her alias based on her parents.

Danny felt he might vomit, thinking back on the times he and Tyler had spent with Ella, oblivious that she was Amelia the whole time. They had gone to parties, done shots, walked across campus swapping stories about classes. But most importantly, she had played Tyler, twirling him around her evil finger.

"Fuck," Danny said, jumping across the room to grab his jacket. He paused to pull the amulet from his desk drawer, too, and shoved it in his pocket. It would be good to see if it had any effect on her. Tyler had mentioned to not worry about anything, but that was precisely what Amelia wanted—a moment of vulnerability. Tyler could die tonight and never see it coming, just like Jason had surely fallen victim under the impression of meeting his girlfriend in the dark, romantic corner of campus.

Danny bolted out of his dorm, slamming the door shut behind him as he sped down the hallway and toward the stairwell, having no time to wait for an elevator. All the research he had done seemed useless in this moment. He needed to get to Tyler as quickly as possible.

When he burst out of the building, the air felt still—too still. The moonlight cast a bright glow, kissing the treetops and sidewalks, thin, transparent clouds gliding across the landscape. Around him, the sound of a thousand whispers exploded in his ears. Danny spun around to see if anyone was nearby, and found the campus only had a couple of stragglers moseying about. He debated calling someone at the security office to come over for backup but decided that would take too much time. He broke into a sprint for Tyler's dorm, pumping his legs, his muscles overtaken by adrenaline.

Danny tried to not think about the fact that he was running to save his best friend's life.

28

Danny Espinoza was definitely onto her, and Ella didn't know how long she had before he revealed her for who she really was. Stories of witness protection would only go so far. If they found her parents' names and dug into Amelia's family tree, they'd find Ella Jones staring back at them. The last thing she needed was any of this being figured out before she'd finished her work. Now, time was of the essence and it meant that killing Tyler had to happen tonight. It just required Ella to seduce him, and in anticipation of the event, she'd bought a revealing outfit that was low-cut on top, short on the bottom. She'd even practiced walking in the high heels she'd bought to go with it. It had only been a coincidence that he'd finally got up the nerve to ask her on a proper date, even if it was just dinner in his dorm room.

Some of the shadows had been tasked with patrolling the house, while the others would monitor the perimeter of the dorms. There wouldn't be time to rid the world of the meddlesome Danny Espinoza. Tyler was the primary target and once she got the revenge she so desperately sought, she supposed she'd simply fade away into that restful, slumbered darkness of eternal death.

She took her time dressing and putting on her makeup. This mortal coil had been enthralling for the short time she'd been in Denver, and she wondered if she'd miss it. The shadows were growing more adept now, able to manifest fully into corporeal humanoid shapes. This gave Ella more help, and she wondered then that if the shadows could become solid, could she become an ethereal shadow and disappear in wisps and tendrils of smoke? Looking into the mirror at her deep maroon lips and black dress, rouged cheeks and lined eyes, she smiled. It would have to be something she tried at some point. She drew in a deep breath and left the bathroom, grabbing her handbag. Inside it, she had two pairs of handcuffs, her knife, and two longish pieces of rope to use on his ankles. "Anything else I might need?" she asked the shadows before she left for the campus.

The shadows only murmured in response, leaving Ella free to head to Tyler's dorm.

Parading herself in front of the residents of Tyler's dorm wasn't particularly difficult. As she walked by, every male turned his head and most said hello. By the time she made it to Tyler's door, it surprised her she didn't have a trail of them following her, though a few heads peeked out of rooms, probably to see which room she was going to. All the more reason she had to kill him quietly, then leave without rousing too much suspicion. They would find his body sometime the next day, and by then, she'd be long gone. Not even a trace.

She fought back a laugh and knocked on the door.

Tyler answered wearing a clean pair of jeans and a buttondown shirt. When he saw her, he visibly gulped, almost sending Ella into a fit of laughter. *Males—they are so predictable*, she thought.

"Hey," he said, motioning her into the room. It was

cleaner than she remembered it. "I was thinking we could order from the local Chinese restaurant." He closed the door.

"That sounds great," she said, not giving it much thought. She wasn't there to eat. Well, not Chinese anyway. "You really cleaned up. Are they giving you a new roommate?"

"Probably not until the beginning of next semester would be my guess. So I have this place to myself for a couple more months," he said, his voice harboring a nervous edge to it. "I grabbed a menu."

She smiled and took it from him. They decided on some sweet and sour chicken, along with spicy mushroom beef and fried rice. Then they waited until dinner came, making painful small talk. Ella didn't want to make her move just yet.

They ate and talked about classes. Tyler telling her how he had no idea what kind of career he wanted and Ella agreeing. "No one I know over the age of forty-five is in the same career or line of work they went to school for," she said with a shrug. She didn't know if it was true, but she'd heard it in passing among college students at least.

The bloodlust began growing within her. How long would she have to wait? She took a measured breath and got up from the desk chair to move beside Tyler on the bed.

He paled slightly and chaffed his hands against his jeans. "What?"

She smiled and laughed, then leaned in and kissed him, not pulling away when the wretched animal put his tongue in her mouth. Pulling away briefly, she began unbuttoning his shirt.

He put his hand over hers. "Are you sure you really want to do this?"

Now she had to reassure him. "I wouldn't be doing it if I didn't want to," she whispered.

"I mean, you're really sure?"

She laughed again. "I'm sure. Are you?"

He swallowed again. Hard. "Okay. This is really going to happen."

Ella finished undoing the buttons on his shirt. "How about I take the lead?" She stopped unbuttoning his shirt and went to her purse, pulling out both sets of handcuffs and the keys. "I get to tie you up."

His expression was priceless. Part disbelief, part excitement, part fear. It was the fear part that Ella liked most. "That's a bit kinky," he said.

"Yeah, but fun kinky," she countered, giving him a lascivious grin. "That way I'm the one calling the shots and you don't have to worry about whether or not I really want it."

The look of disbelief faded, and he took off his shirt. "Okay. I'm game."

She slid back to the bed and kicked off the despicable high heels, then pushed Tyler back onto the bed, her lips pressed to his, her hands exploring his chest. Once she had him pinned down, she handcuffed his left hand to the head of the bedframe. She continued kissing him and handcuffed his right hand to the bed. Her lips and tongue trailed down his neck, causing him to gasp. Ella moved further down to his chest, making her way to just below his navel.

He closed his eyes as she removed his shoes and socks, unfastened the button on his jeans, unzipped them, then pulled them off, along with his boxer-briefs. Her fingers lightly danced across his flesh, causing his erection to dance. She licked the precum from the head of his penis, and giggled.

Tyler watched as she got up and brought back the rope from her purse. She held them up with a sly smile. "I can't forget to tie up your ankles. I want to make sure I can have my way with you without legs and arms getting in the way."

"Uh huh," he said, watching her every move.

She used the soft rope to tie his legs slightly apart, then

slid her hand between his legs to caress his scrotum. *The penis and scrotum will come off easily*, she thought. Ella realized then that she was only missing two things. A gag and the knife. "We need something else." She got up and palmed the knife.

On the desk, next to the lamp, was an old rag he'd pulled from his desk to wipe up sweet and sour sauce, she grabbed that, bent down and kissed Tyler full on the lips again, then pulled away and pushed the rag into his mouth. "You have to be quiet. I don't want people to know we're fucking in here. They'll try to listen."

He said something, muffled by the rag in his mouth.

Ella giggled, opened the knife behind her back, then revealed it. "You see," she said, "I've been waiting to do this for months now."

His eyes went wide with confusion, then terror as he registered the truth and she sliced the skin about an inch under his left breast. It wasn't a deep cut, more a superficial wound.

"Do you have any idea how much work went into tracking you down, becoming Ella, and getting close to you? But it's all been worth it. Every irritating, annoying moment for this." She dragged the blade lightly across his skin, making sure not to cut him. With her other hand, she grabbed his quickly waning erection and began rubbing him while simultaneously dragging the knife to his inner thigh. "Jason was merely a means to an end. Shame he had to die, but these things can't be helped. It's too bad I couldn't slip Danny in there."

Amelia cocked her head to one side, her eyes wide. It felt good being able to drop the Ella act. "Did you have any last words?" A sly grin slid across her lips.

Tyler's body stiffened, and he pulled against restraints in futility.

"I guess not. Let's get started then, shall we?" She leaned

over and licked the thin stream of blood trickling from the cut on his chest. "Mmm. Tastes good."

Holding the blade fast in her right hand, she took it down between his legs, taking up his scrotum and penis in her other hand. "I'm going to enjoy cutting these off before I disembowel you, and I've taken a liking to eyes. They're delicious." Tyler let out a muffled scream.

Then she made a small incision on his inner thigh, mere inches from his manhood.

Something rustled against the window. It was so loud that even Tyler, in his panic to get free, glanced toward it. Outside, it sounded like a thousand voices trying to get into the building. Amelia knew exactly what that meant. Someone was coming, and the shadows were trying to warn her. But she wasn't done yet. She still had a job to do. Again, she gathered up his scrotum and penis and placed the blade against the base.

There was a loud noise in the hallway, a thud, and the door flew open. In burst Danny Espinoza. Amelia jumped up, her lips contorting into a scowl, her eyes wide.

"Get away from him!" Danny put himself between Tyler, still naked and helpless on the bed, and Amelia and her knife. There was something about him that repelled her. Then she noticed something in Danny's right hand. It was black, small, and round, and it terrified her.

She stepped back toward the window. The shadows were still rustling outside, beating the window like a thousand bird wings. The window opened. She glanced over, seeing the shadows beckoning her.

"Jump!" they shouted.

But I haven't finished, she thought, lunging toward Danny with the knife. He dodged her and held out his arm with the black stone in it.

Her stomach twisted violently. "What witchcraft is this?"

"Yeah, that's it," Danny said. "Witchcraft."

Amelia turned and took a run for the window, diving out. She felt the breeze around her body as she sailed toward the ground. Hitting the grass below knocked the wind from her. Laying there for a moment, she didn't dare move. It was as if she could feel eyes on her. Then she heard Danny say, "She's on the ground. Not moving. Knife still in her hand."

"Get up, Amelia!" the shadows closing in on her screeched. "Come with us."

She pressed her eyes closed, willing herself away from her physical form into a translucent black shadow. When she opened her eyes, she realized she was floating, and the shadows were still around her.

"Come," they beckoned.

Amelia joined them, slipping into the dark places, and vanishing into the night where no one could ever find her.

29

Holy shit! Tyler thought, jerking his arms and legs to free himself from the restraints. He looked down to see thin lines of blood still seeping from the wounds Ella had carved. The rag tasted musty, like it had come from a bucket sitting in storage for the last five years. The flavor made him gag, but he'd fought off the escalating urge to vomit to avoid choking on his own puke.

Danny had rushed to the window, gasping for breath as he gazed outside. He spoke in short bursts, taking deep inhales between sentences. "She's on the ground. Not moving. Knife still in her hand." Tyler knew Danny wasn't in the best shape, and his mad dash across campus had likely been the most he'd run since high school gym class.

Tyler mumbled, hoping Danny would get the hint to come untie him and get the damn rag out of his mouth. His friend spun around, saw Tyler's privates flapping around, and glanced away as he approached the bed.

"Ella *is* Amelia," Danny explained as he untied Tyler's ankles. "I can't believe the timing of all this—she was going to kill you. I just had a feeling that I needed to do more research, that something was right in my face, and sure enough I found this connection. I'll tell you more about it later, but first we have to get down there and tie this crazy bitch up."

He finally reached for Tyler's mouth and pulled out the rag, tossing it aside.

Tyler swallowed a mouthful of air, sticking his tongue in and out to wipe the nasty taste away. "I can't believe you're here. I don't know what the hell happened. We were having dinner, then she started rubbing me all over and talking dirty. Next thing I know, I'm tied to the bed, and she pulls a knife on me. It hurts so fucking bad!"

Danny nodded, examining the cuts across Tyler's chest and thigh. "I'm sure, but it doesn't look like she cut any major arteries. We'll get you to a hospital, but we have to get to her first."

"And put her where? We need to hurry before someone else finds her. Who knows if someone else below saw her jump out—it might already be too late."

Danny uncuffed Tyler's hands and untied his bound ankles, and Tyler promptly rolled off the bed and fumbled for his underwear, not able to put his clothes back on soon enough. The two hurried back to the window.

"No fucking way!" Danny yelled. "No!"

Tyler followed his gaze to the ground below, seeing an imprint in the grass where Amelia's body had fallen, but no sign of her. They looked around, hoping to catch her moving through the shadows, but they knew it was too late. If they weren't there to see her get up and leave, then they'd never know to where she had vanished.

"Dan, what do we do?" Tyler asked, grateful to be alive, but horrified that this nightmare still had no end in sight.

Danny shook his head, jaw hanging as he continued to stare outside. The open window let in a strong draft, but neither of them noticed, too occupied with fear. He remained silent, not speaking as his brows furrowed in deep thought. "She's gone, isn't she? We're never going to see her again."

Tyler knew that couldn't be further from the truth, but kept quiet. Amelia might be gone for the moment, but she'd be back, and always would be until she killed him. He scrambled back into his jeans, ignoring the superficial cuts. "Let's go look outside, just to be sure."

He shuffled toward his bed, the sheets a tangled mess of sexual foreplay and attempted murder, and crouched down to reach under, pulling out a long backpack. Tyler unzipped it as Danny watched, fishing out a hammer, three chef knives, and a baseball bat.

"Are you kidding me?" Danny asked. "You were about to be killed with that bag of goodies directly below you. C'mon, Ty."

Tyler let out a nervous laugh, the irony having already settled in. "I know, no need to rub it in. Let's see if we can track her down."

He knew Amelia would never allow herself to be caught out in the open—she was probably already off-campus—but Tyler still wanted to do something productive. Sitting around the dorm and moping would lead them nowhere. At some point, they'd have to return to their research, and make plans to hunt her down. It was best they found her before she found them again. Amelia's thirst for revenge would have only been strengthened by this close call, and they could only trust that her sights were now set on a swift murder—no more time toying with Tyler.

Danny went back to the window, perhaps hoping their eyes had played tricks on them—it was plenty dark outside—but he shook his head and returned to Tyler, his hand outstretched for one of the knives. "I have a bad feeling, Ty. This was too close of a call. And not just tonight, the whole thing. She was playing us from the start of the semester and we had no idea. She could have killed us at any time. All those parties we went to, she could have lured us to a quiet bedroom and finished us. I can't believe I was in her house. If she had come home, I'd have had no chance of leaving that place. We have to be more careful about who we let into our life."

"I agree, but this wasn't even really in our control. I didn't pick Jason as my roommate. *She* found the way to get close to us, taking whatever opportunity she could. How did we not recognize her? That's what I've been trying to figure out."

"All we've had were black-and-white photos from the 1920s. Blurry, grainy photos that only gave us an idea of what she looked like. Bring her to today's world with new fashion, makeup, and a haircut—we never had a chance. We just have to be careful. Where will she show up next? A classmate sitting next to you? A coworker? We still don't fully know what she's capable of. She can change her hair color, her entire look."

"I think we'll know better now. Souls can recognize another soul—I trust my instincts now that I've spent time with her."

Danny let out a soft chuckle. "Ty, she has no soul. Don't fool yourself. Let's go out and have a look."

Tyler slipped his t-shirt back on, grimacing as his movements stretched his skin and the fresh wounds on his chest. The pain was bearable, but uncomfortable. He'd be able to push through as long as his life was at risk.

They left the dorm room, remaining silent as they made their way down the hallway and to the stairwell. They passed a couple of residents who brushed up closer to the hallway walls when seeing the glint of the knives, Tyler and Danny paying them no attention.

Tyler knew how they looked, strolling out of the building

like two crazed men, but the truth was they had survived. *He* had survived.

They stepped outside and the cold air slapped them across the face, tingling the cuts beneath Tyler's shirt. The wind picked up and howled, dead leaves rolling across the sidewalks, crunching beneath their footsteps as they rounded the building toward the front where Amelia had landed.

"She was right here," Danny said when they reached the grass, hurrying toward the spot. The grass had already turned yellow thanks to autumn, but the imprint of Amelia's body darkened a silhouette of her head, splayed arms and legs, and torso. Danny squatted to examine the ground, looking around for signs of any footprints. "She went that way," he said, pointing to the opposite corner of the building.

Tyler followed a couple of soft footprints that faded after a couple of steps, but there was no mistaking the direction they had gone. "That doesn't tell us much. Once she got to the other side of the dorm, it's all pavement. She could have gone any way from there. Do you think she'd go back to her house?"

"No. That place was clearly set up for her to leave at a moment's notice. She doesn't have possessions, no need for her to get anything."

"Do we call that cop? Tell him what happened tonight?"

Danny shrugged. "I don't think Amelia will show her face around here anymore—too risky now that we know who she really is. I can file a report with the security office, let them know she tried to attack you and fled. We'll have to fudge some details to avoid the police, but this way we'll receive alerts if she comes back to campus." He looked at Tyler's shirt, blood seeping through. "Do you need to go to the hospital?"

"No. I think I'm fine." He paused and felt his chest, then swept his hand across his inner thigh. It appeared both wounds had already stopped bleeding. Let's just call Sheriff Abbott and let him know. I'd think Amelia will try to return to her hometown."

"She will, I don't doubt it. All we can do now is stay alert and try the ritual I've been reading about. Impossible to know if it will work, but we have to try. Let's get things together. Are you ready for a long drive?"

Tyler nodded.

They gave up on finding Amelia or dealing with police and security, and after getting what they needed, got into Tyler's car and headed back to Ridgeway where an uncertain future awaited.

❧ 30 ❧

Sheriff Abbott's phone went straight to voicemail for a third time, so Danny hung up. They'd already left him one message. There was no point in trying to leave more. The night before, they'd stopped just outside Ridgeway at a small motel to get a few hours of sleep, having decided they both wanted to be alert before confronting Amelia at her gravesite. Not to mention she somehow didn't seem *as* threatening in the daylight. Having overslept, it was just past three in the afternoon when they reached the Doss family cemetery. Danny was confident there was still plenty of daylight to do the ritual.

"Why did we have to come back here?" There was fear in Tyler's voice. The grave of Amelia Doss had since been filled back in, even though they'd heard from Sheriff Abbott that the grave had been dug up and the bones taken. *Taken, my ass,* Danny thought.

"We have to do the ritual over her grave," Danny told him. Then he handed the amulet to Tyler. "Put this on."

Tyler slipped the black tourmaline over his head and ran his fingers over the stone. "What is it?"

Danny looked over at his friend and said, in a rather serious tone, "It's a stone that will protect you from evil spirits."

"What about you?" Concern washed over Tyler's face, and his eyes darted to the graffiti laden headstone of Amelia Doss.

"Amelia Doss wants to kill you, not me," he said. Not that he wanted to throw it in Tyler's face that he'd been right about Ella, but then this wasn't the time to say, *I told you so.* He just hoped that Tyler believed him now and knew that Danny was just trying to look out for him.

"Yeah, but it seems she kills my friends, too." Tyler glared at Danny. "You should have gotten yourself one of these."

"Hopefully, after today, neither of us will need protection amulets anymore," he said, opening the book. *Intent*, he told himself. *Focus.* It was almost three in the afternoon. It felt a little safer doing this during the day.

"Are you sure this is going to work?" Tyler looked around the clearing, his eyes stopping at the Doss family graves on the other side of the open space. "Do you think she'll show up here and try to kill us?"

"If she does, I have some strong magic in store," Danny said, not feeling as sure as he sounded. "We know she's a devil, and these books have rituals for getting rid of devils."

"But what if they don't work?" There was a hint of panic in Tyler's voice.

Danny surmised his friend was probably suffering from PTSD and would likely benefit from counseling. Hell, Danny had been considering counseling himself. His own run-ins with Amelia Doss had been enough to keep him looking over his shoulder, too. The nightmares, however, had been the worst part of it. Sometimes he would just wake up in a cold sweat, his heart pounding, and *know* that he'd had a run in with Amelia. He wondered if Tyler had experienced this, too.

"If they don't work, next time we hire an actual witch to do the rituals."

"I don't know. Isn't this how we ended up in this mess..."

"Tyler," Danny cut him off. "The longer we spend talking about this, the longer it's going to take to finish. We need to get it going. We'll be losing daylight soon and I don't know about you, but I'd like to be long gone before dusk hits."

Tyler nodded, wrapping an entire hand over the stone around his neck as if clutching it for dear life. Danny hoped it worked like the witches told him it would. After careful consideration and much research, he'd chosen a simple ritual to send Amelia back to the grave. From his satchel he pulled out the flask of holy water, blessed in the Saint Mary Cathedral. Then he took out a single jar candle. It was simple enough that he'd practically memorized the ceremony and only had the book just in case he forgot anything. There was no way he could screw this up, because first he had to conjure Amelia again before he could send her back.

He lit the jar candle and set it against the headstone. Then he began walking counterclockwise around the entire grave, careful to steer clear of walking on top of it, and repeated the chant, in his mind visualizing Amelia, as Ella, getting trapped in a vortex and sucked back into Hell. "I circle this grave widdershins, to draw Amelia Doss back again!" In his mind's eye, the dirt of the grave swirled around like a black hole, sucking everything about Amelia Doss back into the cursed ground she'd risen from.

"Wait! What?" Tyler's voice threatened to break Danny's concentration. A sudden wind from nowhere burst through the trees.

He ignored his friend's cries, and the wind, repeating the chant again, one for each time he circled the grave. The third time he circled, a loud scream, like the call of a banshee, reverberated in the surrounding forest, echoing in the distance. Then came the words, "I will kill you." They didn't sound human—they came in a low growl, like an animal.

Tyler clutched at Danny's arm, his eyes bulging from his head. The light all around them appeared to be fading into darkness. "Shit, shit, shit! Danny, do something!"

Danny peeled Tyler from his arm. "Trust me," he said. Then he switched directions and began circling the grave clockwise. "I circle this grave sun-wise, never again will Amelia Doss rise!" He screamed the words with conviction, not caring if the entire world heard. The vibration of the words shuddered through his bones. Going around a second time, he screamed the poorly rhyming chant again, still visualizing the vortex sucking her in. He went around a third time, the same words coming from his mouth.

Before their very eyes, the dirt of the grave began whirling, forming a small land spout directly on top of the grave. Danny took a step back next to Tyler, who stood steadfast. The flame of the candle next to the headstone shot up like a flamethrower and right in front of them, Amelia appeared, as Ella. At first, she looked like a ghost, semiopaque, but as the dirt of the grave swirled around her, her form became more solid. With a sneer on her lips, she took two steps toward Tyler and reached out to him.

Tyler didn't budge, and Danny dug in his heels, determined to stand next to his friend.

But Amelia's hand hit something, the amulet around Tyler's neck, and a bright bolt of gold light leapt from Tyler, striking her right in the chest, knocking her back on her ass, into the dirt of her own grave.

"Fuck it," Danny said.

Tyler, wide-eyed, dropped his mouth open, but no sound came out.

He began circling the grave clockwise again. "A wretch in life, a cursed spell, I send Amelia Doss to Hell!" He kept shouting it, visualizing her being sucked back into the earth, as if the grave were quicksand.

Amelia's expression changed to fear.

Danny repeated the chant again and kept circling, but this time, Tyler joined in and said the words, too. "A wretch in life, a cursed spell, I send Amelia Doss to Hell!"

The ground rumbled under their feet, the earth opening beneath Amelia. She screamed, and the ground swallowed her to her waist and continued sucking her in.

They repeated the chant while circling the grave a third time.

Only Amelia's head and both arms were above the dirt now. "I'll be back!" It sounded like she said something else, but the dirt muffled the noise as she slipped back into the grave, the darkness following her, revealing the daylight once again. Just like that, it was over.

"Is that it? Is she gone?" Tyler looked at Danny in disbelief.

Danny imagined his own expression shared that same bewilderment. "Now we have to seal the bitch in."

"Right!" Tyler nodded.

Picking up the holy water, Danny shook some over the grave. "In this grave we seal you! Never again will you break free!"

Tyler joined in again, as if adding a second voice to the spell might make it more effective. They repeated the words together until the flask of holy water was empty.

"Should we put a cross or something on it?" Tyler asked, looking wary when they'd finished.

Danny picked up the book and reviewed the ritual. "No, but for good measure, let's sage her grave." He produced the large sage bundle from his coat, lit it, and waved the smoke back and forth in the air. "All negativity be gone from this place." He wasn't sure if that's what he was supposed to say, but he figured a little improvisation and intent wouldn't hurt. If this didn't seal Amelia Doss in her grave...

Once he finished, he blew out the candle, emptied the hot wax over the grave, imagining it was an extra sealant, then packed up the supplies.

"What now?" Tyler asked.

"That's it."

"And you're sure it will work?"

Danny turned back toward the car and started walking.

Tyler followed. "Did you hear me?"

"I heard you," Danny said, walking faster. "There's only one way it won't work."

"What?"

"No—it's okay because I'm positive it's not the case. The only way it won't work is if she's attached to an object," Danny said. "And we know that's not true. I didn't raise her through an object. She didn't come with an object."

Tyler nodded. "That's true. But what if..."

Danny stopped and spun toward Tyler. "No what-ifs. It's over. We've put her back in her grave where she belongs. We both saw her go in, right?"

His best friend nodded. "Yeah."

"Good. We'll never have to worry about Amelia again." Even Danny wasn't so sure. While they may never have had to face Amelia Doss again in person, that didn't mean the psychological damage she'd inflicted wouldn't live inside both himself and Tyler for as long as they both lived.

They reached the car and got in. Tyler started the car. "Should we at least go say hi to our parents while we're here?"

"Then we'd have to explain why we came home," Danny said.

"We could just say we wanted to surprise them," Tyler suggested.

"What if they had plans?" Danny bounced his eyebrows.

Tyler laughed. "Let's head back to Denver. No one needs to know we were ever here." He put the car in reverse and turned it around, then pulled out onto the highway and headed back toward Denver.

They drove in silence for at least twenty minutes, the rock station playing softly in the background. Finally, Tyler turned to Danny and let out a deep sigh of relief. "I can't believe it's finally over."

Danny nodded, but he couldn't shake the feeling that something wasn't right. He tried to dial the sheriff again, no use. This time he left a message telling the sheriff what had happened. When he hung up, he let out a heavy sigh.

"It's really over," Tyler said.

Danny looked into the side mirror, back in the direction they'd come from. It looked dark and foreboding, like a shadow rising from the mountains behind them. "It's really over," he hesitantly said in agreement.

❧

Continue the story with Salvation: Book Three of the Amelia Doss Series.

Want more Amelia Doss?
Salvation (#3)
Nightfall (#2)
Resurrection (#1)

Andre Gonzalez

Andre Gonzalez is the international bestselling author of the Wealth of Time Series. He writes thriller and horror books after spending many years reading and studying the works of Stephen King and Dean Koontz. Keeping readers up late and their hearts pumping a bit faster than normal is his ultimate goal when cracking open one of his books.

When he's not writing, you can find Andre buried underneath a long to-do list and/or his three hyper children. He and his wife are raising their family in their hometown of Denver, CO.

https://andregonzalez.net/

Audrey Brice

Audrey Brice writes supernatural thrillers, mysteries, urban fantasy, and horror stories filled with spirits, demons, supernatural creatures, and occult practitioners. Her love for storytelling and all things supernatural and paranormal began at an early age. As S. Connolly she writes books about witchcraft and demonology. She writes paranormal romance and steamy romance as Anne O'Connell, and she writes PG13 epic fantasy and tame romance as S. J. Reisner. An award-winning author, she lives along the front range of the Rocky Mountains with her husband and three spoiled house cats.

http://sjreisner.com/

Stand Alone Novels: Dark Prince

www.ingramcontent.com/pod-product-compliance
Lightning Source LLC
Chambersburg PA
CBHW070926190726
48292CB00004B/1119